THE STRANGERS

Published by Purple Pegasus Publishing Inc.,
4199 Campus Drive, Suite 550
Irvine, California 92612
USA

For more information about Purple Pegasus Publishing visit purple-pegasus.com

First published in 2016

"A Hero of Our Times" by Rui Wang, published by arrangement with Rui Wang.
"The Stranger" by Lily Liu, translated by Zhu Hong, published by arrangement with Lily Liu.
"Counting Down the Minutes" by Allan Cho, published by arrangement with Allan Cho.
"The Bug" by Lily Chu, published by arrangement with Lily Chu.
"The House in Avenel" by Jieru Zhou, translated by Ying Alexandra Cao,
published by arrangement with Jieru Zhou.
"The Golden Venture" by Yili, published by arrangement with Yili.
"Flowers Bloom, Flowers Fall" by Ma Lan, translated by Charles A. Laughlin,
published by arrangement with Ma Lan.
"Vacances à Paris" by Christina Yao, published by arrangement with Christina Yao.
"Return to Gander" by Xiaowen Zeng, published by arrangement with Xiaowen Zeng.

Library of Congress Catalog Card Number: 2016931623
ISBN: 978-0-9966405-0-3 (hardcover)
978-0-9966405-1-0 (paperback)
978-0-9966405-2-7 (ebook)
Copy editing by Cynthia M. Keil
Cover design and interior design by: Tony Besné

NINE STORIES BY NINE IMMIGRANT WRITERS
BROUGHT TOGETHER BY ONE CONCEPT

THE
STRANGERS

Edited by Anna Wang Yuan

A Purple Pegasus Publication

CONTENTS

THE
STRANGERS

Stranger of Heaven, I bid thee hail!
Shred from the pall of glory riven
That flashest in celestial gale —
Broad pennon of the King of Heaven
Whate'er portends thy front of fire
And streaming locks so lovely pale;
Or peace to man, or judgments dire
Stranger of Heaven, I bid thee hail.

— James Hogg

FOREWORD

I was born and raised in Beijing, China. In 2006, I immigrated to Canada. The following year, during a trip to California, I bought a copy of *The Best American Short Stories 2007*. I assumed that every single story in that anthology was written by an American author. I held that assumption until I began reading the story "Dimensions" by an author named Alice Munro. Somewhere in the story, there was a character carrying a cup of Tim Horton's coffee in her hand. "Wait a minute," I said to myself in alarm, "is she Canadian?"

I paused my reading and spent a couple of minutes musing upon this discovery in spite of my burning curiosity for the character's fate. Tim Horton's isn't an international name like McDonald's or Starbucks. I would have never heard of it had I never been to Canada. What did this discovery mean to me? I don't know. I just felt a connection with Alice Munro, as if I could understand her better than Americans that hadn't tasted Tim Horton's coffee.

I've read more stories by Alice Munro ever since. In 2014, I was commissioned to translate her 12th book, *The View from Castle Rock*, by Yilin Publishing House. ("Yilin" means "the forest of translations" in Chinese, and Yilin Publishing House is China's most prolific publisher of translation works.) It took me a whole year to accomplish the job, and throughout the time I experienced countless joyful moments when I was able to make connections be-

3

tween Munro's work and my own experiences. For instance, in the title story, Alice Munro re-constructs the journey of James Laidlaw, the first ancestor on her father's side to immigrate to North America. Born and raised in Ettrick Valley, a place described by *Statistical Account of Scotland* in 1799 as "having no advantage," James Laidlaw is a dreamer who is obsessed with the notion of moving to America to own better land. By the time he's sixty, he raises enough fare for him and his younger children to embark for the new world. Barely onboard the vessel, he discovers, much to his astonishment and dismay, that there are Highlanders and Irish among the passengers. *Shouldn't there only be decent Scotsmen on deck?* He couldn't help lamenting, "An evil lot, an evil lot. Oh, that ever we left our native land!"

When he immigrated, he met not only foreigners, but also different kinds of his own people whom he would have never met otherwise. And the second part constitutes an even bigger challenge than the first one. That's my own experience, too.

Upon my arrival in Canada in 2006, I made a resolution to write in English. The difficulty seemed insurmountable, but I convinced myself that it was doable. My argument went like this: suppose I was born in 2006 and began learning English the way a baby would. My language abilities will certainly get better as I grow older. The only decisive factor is how long I'll live.

By this year, 2016, I am into the tenth year of my self-imposed mission. I've learned that learning a new language as a grown-up is much more difficult than as a newborn because an adult could always retreat to the safe haven of their mother tongue.

Writers are minorities. Ethnic writers are a minority within a minority. It is amazing that I have met a number of like-minded writers along the way. When I told them that I wanted to collect stories written in English by ethnic Chinese authors, they generously submitted their works to me. While reading the manuscripts, I once again experienced joyful moments of recognition, association, retrospection, and revelation. I saw myself through every piece of their works.

Rui Wang's "A Hero of Our Times" is a heart wrenching tragedy about how a young man tries to make sense of his life in a senseless time in China's history. Yili's "The Golden Venture", set against the background of the Golden Venture incident in 1993, allows us a glimpse of the fate and mindset of illegal immigrants. Christina Yao's "Vacances à Paris" and Xiaowen Zeng's "Return to Gander" are both about how love is elsewhere as the titles suggest. Lily Chu's "The Bug" is not a typical immigrant story. In fact, it has nothing to do with ethnicity or nationality. It's an intriguing mystery.

I also received three stories which were first written in Chinese and then translated into English. At first, I thought they didn't fit into this anthology because they weren't originally written in English. At that point I had already written about a thousand words for the foreword, and a part of it went like this: "All the contributing writers in this anthology had spent their formative years writing in Chinese. They try to make sense of the new world, as well as the old world, by writing directly in their adopted language." Are those words to be forfeited completely? Well, I had to change my criteria if it excluded good writings. At least I can keep the words, "spent their formative years writing in Chinese," can't I?

Ma Lan's "Flowers Bloom, Flowers Fall" tells stories that happened in China. The way the author juxtaposes different times coincides with my sense of scrambled time when I first landed in North America. Lily Liu's "The Stranger" has two layers of narrative. The outer one embodies the main themes of this anthology, and it ultimately inspired the title of this book. The core layer of the narrative is set in China's Cultural Revolution, which links itself with Rui Wang's story and gave me the idea to group stories with similar themes into mini-anthologies. Jieru Zhou's "The House in Avenel", a short and sweet piece that exuberates the nomadic spirit, instantly reminded me of "The Bug" and "The Golden Venture", which led me to group them together.

The last one that came onto my desk was Allan Cho's "Counting Down the Minutes". It proved to be the biggest challenge to my criteria. Allan Cho was born and raised in Vancouver, Canada, and English is his first language. If I included his piece, I had to completely scrap the part—"spent their formative years writing in Chinese . . . " Once again, I pushed the envelope. What is literature for, anyway? It's for breaking existing boundaries instead of building more.

Everyone struggles with their identity. Writers struggle for an audience as well as for their identity. Minority writers' struggle may be doubled. But as long as we keep going, we may be closer to our goals than we think.

Anna Wang Yuan
Irvine, California
January, 2016

THE STRANGERS

PART 1

*"Once we dreamt that we were strangers.
We wake up to find that we were dear to each other."*

— **Rabindranath Tagore**
Stray Birds

A HERO OF OUR TIMES

by Rui Wang

I was born in Xi'an, China, in the late 1950s. Our city is famous for many things, but as a kid, I only knew of one of them: the city walls. The walls were built in ancient times to keep the city safe from the tribes living in the north. Therefore, they are also called fortifications.[1] The walls stand 40 feet tall, 40–46 feet wide at the top, and 50–60 feet thick at the bottom. The top of the walls are as wide as a two-lane road, but there is no traffic. My mom used to spend afternoons there with me when I was little. I still remember how I would run around, carefree.

I started school when I was seven years old. In those days, parents weren't as nervous about their kids as they are these days. I used to loiter on the top of the city walls after school instead of going directly home. It was always fun hanging around up there. The clouds and the birds all looked much closer than they did when they were viewed from the ground. I often stared at the sky or places in the distance until dusk.

One day, while I was walking idly up there, I felt someone tap me on my shoulder. I looked around and saw Weizhong. Weizhong was my next-door neighbor. He was about a year older than I was. My mom asked him to look after me on my first day of school. He

---

[1] Construction of the first city wall in Xi'an (it was called Chang'an then) began in 194 BCE.

11

promised that he would, but he never did. I didn't blame him. At our school, perhaps at every school on the face of the earth, the most natural thing for kids to do is to play with other kids their age. What my mother asked from Weizhong—to go the extra mile to keep an eye on me—was unnatural.

So, you can imagine how excited I felt when I saw Weizhong behind me.

"What's up?" I asked.

"Can you do me a favor?" Weizhong asked.

"Sure, of course." My heart was racing, but I managed to look calm. "What do you want?"

He stuck his head out to me and asked me to count how many whorls he had.

"Wow, you only have one!" I shouted.

In those days, kids believed, for no reason, that the number of whorls one had on the top of one's head was a sign of power. The higher the whorl count, the better. After I found out that I had two whorls, I had been longing to discover a loser who had only one.

"Are you sure?" He looked up, not surprised, but vexed. This made me believe that someone else had already told him about his whorl count, and he simply didn't want to believe it.

"Yes!" I said firmly. "You can check it out yourself if you want to."

"That's the problem." He sighed.

"Well, it's difficult," I agreed. I'd seen girls use two mirrors to check their haircuts. They place one mirror in front of them and the other in the back. *If only we had two mirrors . . . but how could you manage to check the top of your head?*

"Check again!" Weizhong snapped. He bent down one more time, moving his head toward me.

I stared at his lonely, pathetic whorl. An idea sprang to my mind. Weizhong had a pair of knee-length rain boots. They made him look powerful and distinct on the block during rainy days, and it happened to rain quite a lot that year. While the rest of us had to carefully pick paths with higher elevation and dry ground, Weizhong stomped proudly into deep puddles, making water splash in every direction. I asked my mother for a pair of boots, but she waved me away as if brushing off cobwebs. "Are you crazy?" she asked. "A pair of boots like that could feed us for weeks."

I put my hand gently on top of his head. "Lower, lower, lower, once more," I tried very hard to remain serious. My sneer almost ruined my plan.

He was obedient and lowered his knees all the way down to the ground. His head almost struck the ancient bricks of the city wall.

I solemnly announced, "If you give me your rain boots, you can have two whorls."

"What?" He raised his head and looked up at me in confusion.

I blurted out in a bit of a panic, "I'll tell you and everyone else that I saw two whorls. Lower your head!"

He dropped his jaw in disbelief, and totally ignored my order.

"I can tell everybody that I saw two whorls," I announced again.

His eyes shifted. He finally understood and began calculating.

"Oh, come on." I grew impatient. "Do we have a deal?"

He was still in amazement. In those days, what society expected from us were piety, frugality, grit, and other things along those lines. We were not encouraged to do a lot of thinking by ourselves. Still, parents would be worried if their children didn't have any intelligence. I once overheard a conversation between Weizhong's mother and my own. Weizhong's mother said that she was concerned that her child was a bit slow. In return, my mother said, "Being too sharp won't do him any good, either." I knew instantly that they both agreed that I was smarter than Weizhong.

"How about three?" I raised my offer, "I'll tell everybody that I saw three whorls."

I paused for a moment and waited for a response.

"Four!" I said in a desperate manner. "That's my final offer." Even lies have their limits.

Weizhong struggled off the pavement. "Never mind," his voice was somber. "Thank you, though." He dusted the dirt off his pants and left.

I was left behind, wondering what I could have done better.

I didn't have any meaningful encounters with Weizhong until the summer of 1966. It was a strange and ominous season. Everyone saw dark, heavy rain clouds, but no one could say for sure when it would rain and how terrible it would be.

For those who don't know what the Cultural Revolution was like, I can describe it a little bit from my own perspective. In the summer of 1966, our great leader, Mao Zedong, warned us that a bunch of enemies were undermining the Chinese society. He encouraged us to get rid of the adversaries, but he didn't give us clear guidance on how to recognize them, and therefore left great room for improvisation, suspicion, confusion, and tension. It was a common occurrence for some humble and inconspicuous guy on our block to be revealed as a spy. And who blew his cover? His wife, of course.

Somehow, the kids started calling Weizhong "Little Landlord." At first it sounded like an innocent nickname, but the more I heard it, the more it made sense to me. That nickname explained how his family was able to afford a pair of rain boots. His father worked as a plumber in my father's research institute and his mother worked in a garment factory. On the surface, both his parents were wage-earners and didn't make as much as my parents. But the pair of rain boots were a mystery and the nickname provided an explanation. It didn't take me long to find out that Weizhong's mother was the only daughter of a rich landowner who lived in neighboring Lin Tong County. Of course, after 1949, all privately owned land was taken away by the government. But there was still a possibility that Weizhong's grandfather had stashed away some valuables and secretly passed them to Weizhong's mother.

Every time I heard the words "Little Landlord," an image instantly popped up in my mind. It was so vivid that I thought I saw it with my own eyes—an image of an ugly, shriveled old man digging a hole in the ground and burying a pot of gold. I had never met Weizhong's grandfather, but it didn't stop me from picturing him as a creepy, mummy-like creature.

Still, when I called Weizhong "Little Landlord," I was doing it for fun rather than to make an accusation. I was a jealous little kid, and that was that. I wasn't malicious. Every kid needed a nickname, and embarrassing ones were more fun. Nevertheless, Weizhong grew frightened and started cutting school. It seemed that he took it very hard, which made us find humor in it even more.

Some day in late autumn, I didn't see him at school and I became concerned. That afternoon, I stopped by his place to make sure that he was okay. I stood by his door and started calling, "Hey, Little—"

His mother burst out the door and grabbed me by my collar. Back in the 1960s, there was an article of clothing called a "fake collar" which could be buttoned to a shirt. Instead of washing a collared shirt everyday, people could simply wash the fake collar. When Weizhong's mother grabbed me, I backed away and she tore the fake collar loose from my shirt.

"What?" I was taken by surprise.

"Stop that! Stop calling my son 'Little Landlord'!"

"Oh, wow," I stammered, "I didn't . . ."

"Yes, you did!"

"I didn't mean . . ."

"You meant everything! It was you who started all that!"

"What?" I was genuinely surprised now. "Me? Everyone is calling him that name. I was just copying."

She started ranting. When she spoke quickly, a funny accent was exposed. This reinforced my theory that she was from Lin Tong County. Her accent thickened as her speech picked up speed. I couldn't make out every word, but I got the idea. According to Weizhong's mother, it must have been my father who leaked the confidential information to me. My father was the HR officer at the research institute where Weizhong's father worked. My father had access to personnel dossiers.

"You must have heard it from your father!" She concluded.

"So your father was indeed a landlord?" I found a hole in her story.

She suddenly froze with her hand still on my collar. The dumbfounded expression reminded me of Weizhong.

"So it was indeed you!" she snapped. "You started the whole thing!"

"That's not the point." I glanced at the last button holding my collar to my shirt. "Besides, it had nothing to do with me, really."

"It had everything to do with you!" She put the other hand around my neck, almost choking me. I was so scared that I began screaming uncontrollably, "No!"

In our neighborhood, if a kid screams, an adult must be bullying him or her. The scream would instantly draw a huge crowd of spectators. Their stares would shame the bully and make them

16

leave the kid alone.

"Yes!" she screamed, too. She sounded like a desperate toddler. I felt embarrassed for her.

Our screaming competition quickly drew a huge audience. The news soon spread that my father had access to personnel dossiers. Later that night, people busted our door. They all wanted to know what my father saw in their files. Some people pried for information about others too. My father was deeply vexed. He kept explaining to everyone that he didn't have access to personnel information as easily as they had imagined. No one believed him. The crowd around us got denser. My father's feeble, terrified explanations were overtaken by shouting, arguing, and begging. My vision was blocked. I couldn't see my father, but I could imagine that he was as desperate as a trapped mouse. In order to save my father, my mother grabbed me by my arm and pulled me outside. She beat me up under the street lights. I had never seen her act so cruel toward me. I screamed for dear life, which finally caused the crowd to pour out and gather around me and my mom. My father saw the chance and shut the door.

The next morning, I was so embarrassed that I refused to go to school. My parents didn't force me to go. They were preoccupied with their own troubles. They even forgot to lock our door. Of course, break-ins weren't an issue back then because we barely had anything that was valuable. Anyway, no sooner had my parents left than Weizhong pushed open our door and came inside with a pair of boots in his hand.

"What do you want?" I frowned.

"I am sorry," Weizhong looked at me with sad eyes.

"For what?" I asked. "For your mother? Don't be."

"I heard you were beaten up by your mother," he said.

"It's okay," I blushed a little. "She didn't really hurt me."

"Here you go," he held the boots toward me.

"Uh . . . " I accepted them in spite of myself.

"Well," he scratched his head and fumbled for words. In the end, he just said, "I hope you like them."

Weizhong left. I closed the door and started admiring the boots. I drew the curtains shut and tried them on. To my disappointment, they didn't look as stunning as they did on Weizhong. That maybe had something to do with Weizhong's height. The knee-length boots on him turned out to be calf-length on me, which looked less impressive. Plus, through all the fuss in the summer of 1966, I grew more confused as to whether a pair of good quality boots were desirable or despicable. We should look down upon private assets, shouldn't we? Although, deep down in my mind, I still ached for a pair of awe-inspiring boots.

In the end, I decided to throw the boots into the garbage instead of returning them to Weizhong. It was better for no one to have them.

Six months later, a group of Red Guards stormed into my home.

It was the late spring of 1967. The Cultural Revolution hadn't shown any sign of stagnation. After one round of purging, there would always be another round. If you hadn't been thrown out yet, it only meant that you were safe for the moment.

Panic was overtaking everyone. People were afraid that one morning they would wake up and discover that they had always been enemies of the communist country without knowing it. It was a nightmare because you lost control of who you were.

I had no idea how my father was exposed. There must have been someone who took one good look at the survivors, and blew his cover.

The Red Guards ransacked our home and took my parents

away. At the age of twelve, I was left in charge of my two younger brothers.

Our apartment was confiscated and we were ordered to move into a rundown community. The day I moved in, I found out that Weizhong lived next-door. Their family disappeared from my old neighborhood soon after the screaming match between his mother and me. I had never traced his whereabouts, and here he was, living right next to me.

When Weizhong's mother first saw me, she produced a fervent monologue. It was true that her father owned land in the Old Society,[2] but it was also true that all her father's assets were confiscated by the new government. She bore no grudge because by getting rid of the guilty fortune, she became a proud citizen of new China like everyone else.

Weizhong went outside to check out what was going on. When he saw me, he quickly winked. He patted his mother's shoulder and said, "Hey, Mom! Stop that. He's one of us now."

His mother looked at me in bewilderment. After a few seconds she came to her senses and followed Weizhong inside their home. She slammed the door shut. I was pissed.

In order to survive a tough neighborhood and protect my younger brothers, I began to hang out with a street gang, "The Iron Fists". Looking back, calling them a "gang" was really flattering, because they didn't do anything like gangsters do in the movies. Our neighborhood was too poor to induce any property-related crimes. The only semi-gangster behavior was appointing girlfriends. These "appointments" didn't actually involve the girls. They didn't know

---

[2] In Communist China's terminology, any time before 1949, when the People's Republic of China was founded, was called the Old Society.

and probably would have resented any kind of association with us, which made it even more necessary for us to shout out the lucky boy's name whenever his appointed girlfriend walked by our group.

The leader of our gang was named Doggie Li. "Doggie" was a nickname his parents gave him. In some rural areas in China, it was believed that God might envy human children and therefore take them away from their parents. As a protection, the parents would blind the god by giving their children degraded names. It looked like his parents' trick worked very well and Doggie Li grew into a tall, heavy-built, rough guy. I admired Doggie Li in some ways. He had an aura that only a person from a rough neighborhood could have. He didn't argue with anybody. He didn't waste his time with reasoning. If he didn't like something, he would just resolve it with his fists.

Doggie Li chose a girl named Constitution for himself. As his best friend, I was appointed a cute girl named Little Moon.

Secretly, I thought that Little Moon—a pretty, cheerful, and healthy girl, who was also a native of this neighborhood—was a better match for Doggie Li. Constitution, on the contrary, was slim and melancholy, and was an expatriate like me. I didn't understand what Doggie Li could have seen in Constitution. She was obviously not Doggie Li's type.

Since I had known Constitution from my early years, Doggie Li often asked me questions about her.

"Where did she get her name?" he once asked.

"She was born the day China's first Communist Constitution was enacted," I answered.

"Fancy!" Doggie Li exclaimed.

"Well, I think Little Moon's name is fancier. She must have gotten her name from her round face," I said.

"That's why I appointed her to you." Doggie Li patted me on my shoulder. "She is cute, as cute as you are."

I knew a lot more about Constitution than I let on. I knew that her family came from Beijing and that her father was still in prison. I didn't tell Doggie Li that I used to attend ping-pong school with her, or that I enjoyed listening to her speak in her impeccable Mandarin.[3] I also didn't tell him that I loved to listen to her peals of laughter each time she either won or lost a point in a ping-pong game.

We sometimes picked on a younger or smaller kid and forced him to shout names outside the girls' houses. One day, some of Doggie Li's enforcers grabbed a random kid from the street and dragged him all the way to the building where Constitution lived.

I was surprised when I saw the kid's face—it was Weizhong.

Although Weizhong and I were next-door neighbors, we rarely saw each other. The one-year age difference separated us—he was in middle school and I was still in elementary school. Plus, Weizhong stayed home everyday after school. He had to take care of his mom, who had developed a mental illness. I, on the other hand, would roam the streets with my "gangster" friends.

When I recognized that it was Weizhong, I stepped back and hid behind a corner.

I heard Doggie Li order Weizhong to call out Doggie Li's name under Constitution's bedroom window.

To my surprise, Weizhong flatly refused. I was stunned.

I heard Doggie Li say, "On the count of three, if you don't shout my name, I'll smash you into ground pork. One, two, three!" I imagined that Doggie Li grabbed Weizhong by the collar and raised his fist high in the air.

---

[3] Mandarin is the official language of China.

"Weizhong!"

There was silence and then hysterical laughter.

I heard Doggie Li shout, "Fucking lunatic!" After that, I heard a dull thump.

"You killed him!" A kid screamed. Next, I heard the crowd scatter. I, too, started running as fast as I could, as if I were running for my own life.

That night, I stayed at home, but left the door slightly open. When I heard Weizhong walking by, I opened the door completely. He was surprised to see me.

"Hello," he said.

I looked him over from head to toe. He looked okay except that his head was wrapped in bandages. He held a washing basin with one hand. It looked like he was on his way to the public washroom.

"What?" he asked. "Why the hell are you staring at me like that?"

"What happened to your head?" I pretended like I didn't know anything about the incident.

"Got hit by a fucking lunatic with a brick." He sounded a bit excited. I noticed that there was a fake collar stained with brown spots in the basin.

"Is that blood?" I pointed to the collar.

"Yeah." He looked a bit shy.

"It must have hurt."

"It's okay."

"Glad to see that you are fine."

"Yup, I'm alive." He sounded very pleased with himself.

Weizhong kept the bandages on his head for about a month. He was still small and quiet, but somehow he acquired a menacing air. Even Doggie Li tried to avoid him. Whenever Weizhong passed by, Doggie Li simply looked the other way.

But Doggie Li wouldn't give up that easily.

A few weeks later, Constitution's younger brother began to hang out with us. He followed Doggie Li everywhere. He even followed him to the public restrooms when Doggie Li needed to go. Doggie Li openly introduced him as his brother-in-law and treated him much better than he did the rest of us. After Weizhong got rid of the bandages, someone in the gang took Weizhong out of class and let Doggie Li's "brother-in-law" slap Weizhong in the face while shouting obscenities. I was really surprised by Doggie Li's skill of manipulation. He who had always believed in violence now started to use his brain. I felt threatened. I started to look for a way out. I often pretended to be sick and withdrew from the gang little by little.

I returned to my old habit—wandering all by myself on top of the city walls during the afternoon. The first time I climbed onto the top and saw the estranged scene in front of me, I almost had a heart attack. I saw faraway fields, birds, the sky, and clouds. I felt as if I could merge into the shallow and the deep, the short and the high, the nearby and the faraway.

Please carry me away, to anywhere else and any other time.

One afternoon, while I was shuffling dreamily on the wall, I felt someone tap me on my shoulder. I looked around and saw Weizhong smiling at me.

"Hey, dude. Check it out," he said and stuck his head out to me, a bit elated.

I saw a scar on his head about the size of a penny. It was round in shape, but the edges were ragged, and not a single hair grew out of it.

I understood instantly. "Wow," I said in sheer admiration, "you've made yourself another whorl."

Time flies so fast. Without knowing, we had lived through our youth and became young adults. After several years of the Cultural Revolution, the cities were nearly dysfunctional. The economy was bad and job opportunities were scarce. Almost all new high school graduates became unemployed. At the end of the 1960s, Mao Zedong painted a romantic picture for young people—go to the countryside and work the land. This utopian dream successfully channeled new labor forces to the countryside in the first few years, but by the mid-1970s, the time when I graduated from high school, the rosy bubbles had already burst. Based on the information we gathered from the first group of people who went there, we knew that living in the countryside meant hunger, backbreaking labor, physical abuse, and even rape. But every graduating student had to go, unless you had a damn good reason not to.

I broke my collarbone while wrestling a few years prior. At the time, I thought I must have been the most unfortunate person in the world. Now this injury became my ticket to remain in the city.

Doggie Li was not as lucky. I heard from someone that he cut off his little finger with a kitchen knife. Unfortunately, he was told that he could still do field work with nine fingers. However, he didn't mutilate himself for nothing. He was assigned to the Southern County where there was a vast stretch of plains to make sure that farming was less demanding than in the mountain areas.

"I should have broken my collarbone, too," he told me before leaving for the countryside.

"You could at least try," I joked while glancing at the lonely stump on his hand.

"No guts," he shrugged.

It was the first time that he ever showed a defeated expression in front of me. It was also the last time that I saw him. Life is a magician that changed a notorious bully into an ordinary, dull man.

Among all my old acquaintances, Constitution was the only one who had been sent to the Northern Mountain District. Her father was still in jail due to political reasons, which guaranteed that her family would receive the worst treatment. Besides, their family was from Beijing, and therefore lacked local connections. The Northern Mountain District had the most barren mountains in the whole province. Whoever went there simply could not survive on those meager wages. I was worried about her, but I couldn't do anything about it. I decided to go to the railway station on the day of her departure. I thought that was the least I could do.

At the railway station, I was shocked when I found out that Weizhong was going to the Northern Mountain District too. A light danced in his eyes as his hand stretched out to me for the first time in years.

"Take care, buddy." I grasped his hands tightly.

His eyes wandered behind me. I turned around and saw Constitution. Her eyes were red from weeping and her movements were listless. It was unsettling when I discovered that her delicate beauty still had power over me. I fought my desire to hold her in my arms. Weizhong, however, hurried over and helped Constitution haul her belongings onto the train.

The weeping of parents, sons, daughters, sisters, brothers, and friends was almost deafening. I saw Weizhong find a seat and gesture to Constitution, who otherwise would have stood in the aisle almost motionless. Once Constitution seated herself, a wave of people passing by obstructed my view. The loudspeaker announced the train's departure. An uproar of weeping and shouting shook the ground, drowning even the steam whistles from the nearby giant locomotives. Hands were stretched out of every window, waving and grasping frantically at the air.

Weizhong pushed the crowd and stuck his head out of the window. He waved to me, quite high-spirited.

"You fucking lunatic," I shouted to him, half-amazed, half-teasing.

Later, I found out that Weizhong was the only person in the school who went to the Northern Mountain District out of his own free will. A day's labor down there was worth just eight cents, barely enough to send a letter home. Yet, Weizhong and I started to write to each other anyway. At first, my purpose for writing to Weizhong was purely to receive information about Constitution. I could have written to Constitution myself, but deep down in my mind, I had appointed Constitution to Weizhong. No matter how much I desired her, I couldn't give up my city life and go to the countryside with her. *Weizhong deserved Constitution more than I did.*

Six months later, Weizhong told me he had made friends with a much older student who had a personal library filled with banned books. Socrates, Plato, Aristotle, and Hobbes began to fill his letters. He read Turgenev's *Father and Son*, Dostoevsky's *Crime and Punishment*, Tolstoy's *War and Peace*, and Pushkin's poetry and prose. He simply worshiped Lermontov. During one of his brief home visits, Weizhong showed me a notebook—Lermontov's *A Hero of Our Times*, copied word for word in his own handwriting. He said he was trying to memorize the whole book. At a time when Mao was God and his *Little Red Book*[4] was the gospel, everything else was regarded as ideologically poisonous. Weizhong could go to jail and I could get into trouble for failing to report him to the authorities.

"I simply have to love it because Pechorin says and does exactly what I have in mind but don't dare say or do." Weizhong said.

Grigory Pechorin, an army officer, was depicted by Lermontov

---

[4] *Quotations from Chairman Mao Zedong* was considered the most important book, if not the only legitimate reading material, during the Cultural Revolution. The book is also nicknamed *Little Red Book* because of the color of its cover.

as a fatalist who is brave and reckless, impulsive but calculating, tender-hearted yet cold-blooded. After I read the copied manuscript, I was struck by how Weizhong's hero successfully turned himself into a social outcast. He broke women's hearts and became a reckless rebel against the establishment. I found it difficult to put Weizhong and Pechorin in the same category. Weizhong was kind, careful, and considerate. He would never break anyone's heart, much less a woman's heart.

Strangely, Weizhong's letter was deprived of information concerning Constitution. It made me suspect that Constitution didn't return Weizhong's love at all.

Once, during a heated discussion of Plato's ideals, I asked him whether Constitution could understand what he was referring to. He froze for a second and then murmured, "She has potential."

"What do you mean by that?" I pursued. "Is she your girlfriend or not?"

"Well," he blushed. "Not yet."

"What a shame!" I cried. "You're such a loser!"

I knew perfectly well that Weizhong had been helping and protecting Constitution. I couldn't imagine a delicate flower like Constitution being able to survive the rough environment otherwise. I believed that Constitution owed her life to Weizhong.

"It's okay," he said calmly. "Love is not something to be traded, you know."

"You know what?" I rolled my eyes. "I think reading all these philosophical books made you stupid."

He smiled sheepishly.

A few years later, as the economy staggered back up, factories and companies started recruiting again. The competition was cruel because the amount of young people stranded in the countryside vastly outnumbered the positions available. Several students were literally stabbed in the back by their roommates because they were seen as roadblocks to the city. Nonetheless, fleeing the countryside was the trend. Eventually, everyone who wanted to leave left. What was excruciating was the process—to see others pack up happily without knowing when it would be your own turn.

Weizhong and Constitution belonged to the last group that said goodbye to their settlement houses in the countryside. Constitution obviously didn't have any resources to get herself back to the city sooner. As for Weizhong, according to my understanding, he probably stayed there out of his own free will.

When the paperwork came to the village, it was revealed that Weizhong was assigned to the Meteorological Bureau located in our city, but Constitution could only go to a construction company in Tangshan, a city about 900 miles away. When Constitution heard the news, she locked herself in her room and refused to eat anything.

A switch was arranged in a week. Constitution was reassigned to the City Meteorological Bureau and Weizhong would be a construction worker in Tangshan instead.

The villagers said that Constitution would have died if the new paperwork had arrived half a day later.

Before heading to Tangshan, Weizhong spent two weeks in our hometown, Xi'an. One afternoon, we climbed onto the top of the city walls for a walk.

I asked him casually if he had had any progress with pursuing Constitution.

"No," he said, "I am not pursuing a relationship."

I asked him why. If it weren't for Constitution, why did he make all these sacrifices?

"It's hard to explain," he said. "But trust me, I'm not altruistic. I did everything for myself."

He stuck his head out to me and said jokingly, "Count how many whorls I have."

I pushed his head away. "You thought you were being a hero, didn't you?"

"Yes," he murmured, blushing a little. Then he went back to his usual expression—determined and calm. Pechorin suddenly sprang to life and stood in front of me. I knew that beneath Weizhong's macho and stoic camouflage, there was a volcano of emotions.

A flock of birds were disturbed. They fluttered their wings and quickly rose to the sky. I traced them for a short while, but they soon flew out of sight.

That was the last time I saw Weizhong.

Three months later, an earthquake with a magnitude of 7.8 struck Tangshan and killed two hundred and forty thousand people. Weizhong was one of them.

About half a year later, I met one of Weizhong's former co-workers. He explained to me that Weizhong practically caused his own death. "Most of the workers on our construction site survived because we slept in tents that night," he paused, "Weizhong was a weirdo. He didn't hang out with us. He didn't play cards or drink with us on weekends. When he was not laying bricks, he was either reading or writing. Nobody really knew what he read or wrote."

That was typical Weizhong. I thought.

"He also tried, whenever possible, to skip the daily political meetings. About a month ago, the party secretary asked all of us to vacate the dormitory building and live in tents to experience what it was like for the revolutionary predecessors to live during the war against the Nationalists.[5] Weizhong resisted openly and said it was stupid and futile." He paused. "That's why he was in the building when the earthquake happened. We loved him. Even the party secretary respected him." Weizhong's co-worker continued. "After the earthquake, we dug him out quickly. His body was among the first thousand that were recovered. There were still body bags at that time, and he was buried properly. Later on, the bulldozers simply pushed the bodies into a ditch," he added, as if to console me. "He is resting in peace. He looked as if he were still sound asleep."

I remembered that Weizhong and I had talked about death when we were nine or ten. It was a starry night and we were high up on the city walls. While we gazed upward, I was horrified to think that if we died, we would not have any consciousness of the physical world. "You mean there won't be a tomorrow or a day after tomorrow for us if we die? How terrible!" I mused.

Weizhong was not horrified. "Maybe it's just like going back to sleep, the long sleep we were in millions of years before we were ever born."

Weizhong was twenty-one when the earthquake struck. A few months later, Mao Zedong died and the Cultural Revolution ended. All this happened while Weizhong was asleep, sound asleep.

During the winter of 2009, I traveled from the United States to my hometown for a short visit. The city had expanded greatly since I left years ago. My old neighborhood was gone and new high-rise buildings were everywhere. My friends were scattered all over the city. I traveled across the city every day to visit them. One time at a dinner party, one of my friends mentioned that the city walls had

---

[5] The Nationalists refers to the Nationalist Party of China. It is a political party that governed all or part of mainland China from 1928 to 1949. It is also translated as Kuomintang as it appears in Allan Cho's "Counting Down the Minutes".

become a tourist hotspot.

"Our government has proposed for the Xi'an Fortification to be included in the UNESCO's World Heritage List," one of my friends said.

"The bad news is that everyone will have to pay an admission fee to get on top of the walls and it won't be cheap," another friend added. "I heard that it's around 50 RMB."

"Really?" I said. "I used to go there every afternoon when I was little."

"Let bygones be bygones," the third friend chimed in. He was a little tipsy.

Somehow, I felt a pang in my heart. Ever since I landed in my hometown, I had a feeling that something was missing, but I couldn't figure it out. Now, I painfully realized that I was mourning for Weizhong's absence.

I asked as casually as possible if anyone had Constitution's telephone number. One of my friends made several calls and finally got it for me.

The next day, I picked up the phone and dialed her number.

Constitution was delighted to hear my voice. "Yes, yes," she sounded warmly on the line. "Of course I remember you. We should go out and eat sometime."

At seven o'clock sharp, Constitution appeared at the table I had reserved. Thirty-something years had passed. She had grown from a slim, delicate beauty to a plump, magnificent woman. I had heard that she had married very well and was living a wealthy, carefree life.

She ordered fried scorpions, steamed tortoise, stir-fried frog legs, and a bottle of Coca-Cola. The dishes were all expensive choices, popular among wealthy Chinese customers, but the Coca-

31

Cola seemed a bit childish and out of place.

"You haven't changed," she squinted and sipped her Coca-Cola.

"Nonsense. I am almost bald," I said with a laugh.

"You're wondering why I'm drinking Coca-Cola, aren't you?" She made a grimace.

"Wow," I nodded, "you're sharp."

"I have a Coca-Cola addiction," she explained. "Do you know why my father was thrown into prison during the 1960s? He kept a picture of himself from when he was younger. In the photo, my father is standing on a street, holding a bottle in his hand. He told me the picture was taken in New York. Guess what he was holding?" She stopped and looked at me inquiringly.

"Coca-Cola?" I answered, tentatively.

"Yes."

"And?"

"When he was accused of spying during the Cultural Revolution, the photo was confiscated as a piece of evidence. They thought the Coca-Cola bottle was a code."

"How ridiculous!" I cried.

"The sad thing is that I had no idea what Coca-Cola tasted like during all those dark years. After the Cultural Revolution, when Coca-Cola first appeared in Xi'an's restaurants, my father took our whole family there. We ordered a dozen cans of Coca-Cola that night. I've been addicted to it ever since."

I calculated quietly. I was probably in college at that time.

I grabbed the 2-liter bottle of Coca-Cola and filled my glass to the brim. I raised my glass and said, "Cheers! To surviving!"

"To surviving!" Constitution also raised her glass. I saw tears fill her eyes.

She gulped down the brown fluid in her glass. "I would like to thank you," she said in a serious tone.

I didn't know what to make of her comment.

"Years ago," she continued, "when my family and I were at our lowest point, you stepped in to protect me and my brother."

"What?" I was stunned. "What did I do?"

"You introduced my brother to Doggie Li's gang. You said that would stop Doggie Li from harassing me." She looked at me intensely. "Boy, you are smart. You really are."

I frowned a little. Honestly, I had totally forgotten about that episode. But if that was the way she remembered it, I had to trust her.

"Well," I scratched my head, "well, I don't know how I stumbled upon an idea like that."

Perhaps the memory of the hard days triggered her emotions. I saw pearls glistening in her eyes. They trailed down her cheeks, and left two streaks in her thick makeup.

"Excuse me," she groaned and left hastily.

I guessed that she was going to the powder room, and I was right. When she came back, her face looked smooth again.

"Do you ever think of Weizhong?" I asked.

"Who?"

"Weizhong."

She still looked confused.

"The boy who went to the Northern Mountain District with you. You two were the only students from our school who went down there."

"Oh, that guy. Of course I remember him. He showed me his whorls one day. He told me that he made himself a whorl," she sounded like she thought it was very funny. "How is he doing?"

"You really have no idea?" I was stunned.

"What are you talking about?" She inquired sincerely.

"Do you remember how you ended up in the City Meteorological Bureau?"

"Oh, that! That was another ordeal." She shook her head. "I protested and pretested. I was determined to starve myself to death if I had to. I wasn't kidding. In the end, the authorities caved in and let me go back to Xi'an."

"It wasn't like that," I said. I went on to explain how Weizhong arranged the switch.

"Really?" She repeated this word through my explanation. When I finished my story, she reached out to me across the table and grabbed my right hand. She asked me where Weizhong lived.

"I want to thank him, right now!" Her eyes flashed with eagerness and sincerity. "I want to do something for him if he needs help."

My hand was wrapped by her warm, soft hands, the intimacy I had longed for throughout my adolescent years.

I avoided her eyes. At last, I said, "let bygones be bygones."

She withdrew her hands and picked up her chopsticks. We were eating silently. There was music floating in the air, but I hadn't paid any attention to it. In the silence, I recognized the lyrics. It was Don Mclean's "Vincent".

"This world was never meant for someone
As beautiful as you."

ABOUT THE AUTHOR

Rui Wang was born and raised in Xi'an, China. He received his master's and doctorate degree in the United States. He is currently a professor and the Dean of the University Library at California State Polytechnic University, Pomona. He has also worked and taught at Northwestern University, Binghamton University, Beijing Foreign Studies University, Xi'an International Studies University, and Humboldt State University. Rui Wang is also a novelist, a columnist, an editor, and a filmmaker.

(From left to right) Bei Dao, Yu Hua, and Rui Wang in Eureka, California, 2004

Q & A
WITH RUI WANG

Anna Wang Yuan asked Rui Wang five questions after reading his short story, "A Hero of Our Times".

Q: I have read your novel, *Ta Xiang Gu Guo* (*Mother Country and Other Countries*. Beijing: China Friendship Publishing Co., 2008) and I think that your short story, "A Hero of Our Times", shares the same perspective as your novel, a perspective through which a weathered, middle-aged immigrant looks back at his childhood spent in his mother country. Wei Su commented that your novel expressed the theme of "transcendence and salvation."[6] Was the theme, "transcendence and salvation" what you had in mind when you wrote "A Hero of Our Times"?

A: No. I doubt my mind ever went there. "A Hero of Our Times" is actually based on a true story. The main character, Weizhong, was my childhood friend, and when we were young, the times we were living in simply did not allow us to grow up naturally. He was a very ambitious boy, but had to leave this world so early. I often wonder what he would be like if he were still with us.

---

[6] Wei Su, "A New Perspective Gained from Displacement and Juxtaposition—An Introduction to *Ta Xiang Gu Guo*" (*Mother Country and Other Countries*. Beijing: China Friendship Publishing Co., 2008)

Q & A

Q: You quoted Gustav Mahler at the beginning of your novel, "I am three times homeless: a native of Bohemia in Austria; an Austrian among Germans; a Jew throughout the world—always an intruder, never welcomed."[7] My takeaway from this quote is a sense of exile. As an immigrant, due to your change in citizenship, do you share the same frustration as Gustav Mahler?

A: The publisher of my Chinese novel used a quote from Gustav Mahler, an Austrian composer, which, interpreted by many readers, questions citizenship. In my view, citizenship is overrated because it really doesn't help in so far as to define anyone's character, education, profession, or anything else. Citizenship matters much less than the specific community a person belongs to. However, ethnicity matters somewhat. For instance, if you look like a Chinese person, you will most likely be treated as one.

Q: Please tell me more about your writing. As a professor and administer, you must write in English on a daily basis. Why do you also want to write stories? Do you feel comfortable writing stories in English? Are there any challenges in terms of language?

A: True. At work I have to use English all the time. I speak at meetings and hold or participate in various discussions. I write emails and all kinds of notes and memos. I rarely write stories in English. "A Hero of Our Times" was at first meant to be non-fiction, but then morphed into a short story, thanks to encouragement from you guys. I believe I can write stories in English without many problems, if I can somehow get into the mood, by which I mean if I have a strong urge to write one. I personally don't think language is a problem. But if I'm asked to translate a story I wrote in Chinese into English, I probably would find that much more

---

[7] (Alma Mahler, *Gustav Mahler:Memories and Letters*)

difficult, because I believe certain concepts are most appropriately expressed in the language which gave birth to those concepts. Examples include filial piety, left-over girls (Sheng Nu), etc., which are generated in Chinese culture in the first place and can hardly be translated into other languages.

Q: Please tell me your favorite English writer(s).

A: When I was learning English as a kid, I read almost all the works by the Brontë sisters. I grew to like them, though at the time I found them dark, and at times dreary. Later, I grew very fond of Carol Shields, who wrote *The Stone Dairies*. I read every single book she wrote and highly recommend her to you. I also like Jhumpa Lahiri.

Q: If you could choose freely, which country would you prefer to live in?

A: China, though I hope I can travel to other countries from time to time.

THE STRANGER

by Lily Liu
Translated by Zhu Hong

We often ran into each other on the bank of the Fraser River, sharing a bench as we watched the setting sun, to be followed by dusk. I was drawn to her face as it reflected the fading light, her face with its fleeting shades of melancholy, one moment breathing resentment, then softened by an understanding, it seemed, of the vagaries of life itself.

So far we had never spoken to each other, a smile had been our only form of greeting. "Interested in a sip of Dragon Well tea?" She placed an exquisite tea set on the stone table near the bench. It seemed that our long-standing wordless communication had reached an end, and this was the start of a new friendship. She carefully extracted a thermos flask from her bag. "I filled it as I was leaving; now the water is just the right temperature to soak the tea."

"You live nearby, I suppose . . ." Having settled in the West, I have come to respect other people's privacy. I was not probing, just making small talk.

She smiled without replying.

Meticulously she poured out the tea, and immediately the elusive fragrance of Dragon Well tea was wafted in the light evening breeze. I savored the tea, as I studied the woman by my side. Could I say that "her best days are over" and that she was "clinging to the remnants of her beauty?" No, she did not fit that stereotype. True, she was no longer young, the crow's feet on either side of her temples gave away her age. Moreover, the quiet resignation lingering in her gaze revealed her to be a woman with a past, but her movements as she poured out the tea were graceful. No, she was not a frivolous woman. Of medium height, she carried herself with dignity; her clothes were of elegant cut, the colors were muted and well-matched, revealing an artistic temperament. She had a smile on her face, a friendly smile, not over done, just enough to show that she was an easygoing person.

"I suppose we can say that we have known each other for a while, though we have never spoken," she murmured as she sipped her tea. At least three times a week, I would sit here to watch the setting sun. In the distance, the mountains seemed to close down on the river, which flowed quietly, rarely disturbed by the stormy weather. As I watched the sun's orb fade away beneath the last gleam of the sunset, I would be gripped by a turmoil of feelings. Right in front of me, on this side of the river, however, people were frolicking on the bank, putting behind them the fatigue of the day.

Well, I must say it is providence, this thing that draws people together. People run into each other by pure chance. To think of all the people that have passed by this bench, usually to take a break from their walk; they nod, say hello, and pass on. Probably she and I, due to some perverseness, both struck to this same bench and at the same hour. I thought it was funny. She on her part, however, now lost her cool and could not hold back her words. Thus, before we went through the preliminaries to break the ice, she dug right into her story.

Daylight hours are longer here in Vancouver, so dusk arrives later than usual in the summer. The water in the Fraser River is uniformly calm, disturbed only by light ripples, while the mountains in the distance look down silently. At dusk, however, the quietness of the bank is broken by sounds of people; people walking, people running, though everyone keeps to his or her own space. The liveliness of people on the riverbank seemed to have dispelled some of the melancholy in her eyes. Although I knew nothing about her, I was sure that there was a story behind that emotional showing.

I do not remember how she began her narrative, all I know is that the moment she mentioned the year 1966, it had unwittingly touched off my own images of that maniacal time and age; a deeply hidden wound was opened, and out poured a flood of memories.

A college graduate who returned from overseas that majored in Western classical music, and a music teacher at a high school—those titles alone were enough to seal my fate. She told her story numbly, as if talking about a dead and buried past. Or perhaps the enduring love which she had clung to all through those years had swept away the memory of suffering shared by all.

"At the time, I had graduated from a musical school in New York and had started teaching music at a middle school in China. It was barely a year before the Cultural Revolution happened—I was ready to embrace the Cultural Revolution. Wasn't it supposed to be a great and glorious event . . . ?"

Of course! Wasn't I, just turned thirty, equally excited and ready to throw myself into the movement? Innocent, passionate, blind—that was what our generation was like. Hadn't I myself renounced my Canadian passport without a second thought, the passport to another world? Passion was dashed by cold reality, and then I had a lifetime to savor the price that I had to pay for my youthful recklessness.

"I was reveling in the embrace of my motherland, or so I thought, when the storm broke and swept me up in its wake . . . . I had no family with me in China. As for friends and colleagues, they had turned into strangers overnight . . . ."

The tea in my cup had turned cold and left a bitter aftertaste in my mouth.

Tears welled up in her eyes, but she held them back, while the fingers wrapped around her tea cup shook slightly. "I don't blame them—in those times, it was each for himself; no one wanted to be contaminated by being in contact with me. They were in distress too. Even though they actually sympathized with me, what could they do?"

I had lived through the same hell. I understood her feelings perfectly.

"I fell in love. He was an art teacher, our shared fate led to mutual sympathy, and then to love . . . ."

Was she muttering to herself? Or was she talking to me? Her account of the affair was so brief, without the wordy protestations and violent promises of undying love. I suppose this is what we mean by the bittersweet memories of past pain.

"It was during the worst of times, when love was forbidden, but suffering was shared, that I was with child," she kept her voice steady, but could hardly keep out the pain throbbing underneath.

I held my breath, afraid to disturb her as she relived her past life in her motherland; when two broken hearts had joined together while being battered by storms.

"We did not have legitimate status, thus no right to express our feelings, not to mention the fact that we were targets at the time. He did not live through the cruel struggles, he exhausted his own life to draw his last painting. The blood sparkled in the sunlight, his blood, which was splattered on the pavement when he threw himself off the rooftop. He died immediately, and I did not have the right to weep."

The gleam of the sunset peeped out from under the gathering clouds of dusk, and lit up the Fraser River.

"Later, there was a change in policy, I was allowed to come back to Canada and visit my father, who was seriously ill. There I gave birth to our son, a child who would never see his father. I live for my child. It is the image of the father living through the son that sustains me in my wandering life." Her voice was calm. Dashed against the rock of fate, her heart had become deadened to pain, like a pool of still water. But her story, as she told it, still fell on my heart like a battering rock.

I had been through that hell myself. I lost count of what she was saying as my own thoughts flew back thirty years, to that time when I was deliberating at death's door, when death had seemed more merciful than life. My best friend had held me back, saying, "No matter what, you got to live it down for the sake of the children. Just think of yourself as a maid to the children." It was under those circumstances that I dejectedly took the children and flew across the Pacific, following in the steps of my forbearers. I decided that my life had ended during those terrible years, and all I had left to live for were the children.

"Although I was provided for by my father's inheritance, being a single mother and still young, I was urged to marry. So I became the second wife of a businessman from overseas. It was a marriage without love, we just got together for the sake of forming a family. We respected each other and kept a distance, and three years later, we ended that stifling relationship. I suppose love is possible only once in your life—that once should be enough to sustain you throughout your life. I became a piano teacher and tried to snatch the remnants of my life through music. Due probably to his father's genes, my son has loved drawing since childhood. It seems that his father's life is rekindled in him; he is now a painter with a growing reputation . . . ."

For a brief instant, I had tried to interrupt to ask for her son's name. She seemed to have noticed, and gently shook her head, and I did not pursue her with the question.

I suppose every life is unique, each with its own story, but it would be satisfying to have truly loved once.

In the deepening sunset, tufts of clouds darkened, some melted away, while others stretched out like arms trying to hold back the sun. As the day drew to a close, however, the glory of the sun as well as the shades of the darkening clouds were all wrapped up and disappeared in the gloaming. We sat silently, each lost in our own thoughts. The sights and sounds of people on the bank had receded along with the setting of the sun. My own thoughts had long since raced through the dark tunnel of time and I was reliving those events that took place on that vast and ancient land . . . .

"Are you OK?" A voice full of concern shook me out of my reverie on the other side of the Pacific. I looked up and saw a blue-eyed, golden-haired jogger. Only then did I see that the tea set on the stone table was gone. She had left. I could barely make out her contours in the deepening gloom, and I had never asked for her name or address. I did not see her the next day, neither did I see her the next week, nor the next month. The mountains and the river were still there, but her shadow never again fell on the long bench. Sometimes, I think I catch sight of her fleeting shadow, but it is always just an illusion.

She was right, we do not need to have known each other; it

THE STRANGER

was just providence. She may have been speaking to herself, or she may have been pouring out to a stranger, whatever it was, she had finally managed to open the window of her soul.

ABOUT THE TRANSLATOR

ZHU HONG is a prolific translator and a visiting professor who teaches courses on post-Mao writing in the department of Modern Foreign Languages and Literature at Boston University. She is the editor and co-translator of *The Stubborn Porridge* (Braziller, 1994), *Festival of Flowers—Essays by Contemporary Chinese Women Writers* (Yilin Press, 1995), *A Frolic in the Snow* (Liaoning Educational Press, 2002), *China 1927: Memoir of a Debacle* (MerwinAsia, 2013), *Will the Boat Sink the Water?: The Life of China's Peasants* (Public Affairs, 2005), *The Serenity of Whiteness: Stories by and about Women in Contemporary China* (Ballantine Books, 1992), *The Chinese Western: An Anthology of Short Fiction from Today's China* (Ballantine Books, 1991), and *A Higher Kind of Loyalty* (Pantheon, 1990). Her translations of short stories from Chinese have appeared in *The Antioch Review, The Chicago Review, The Paris Review,* and *The Iowa Review.*

LILY LIU is a former editor at the Institute of Foreign Literature in the Chinese Academy of Social Sciences. She has continued her writing, editing, and translation work ever since she immigrated to Canada in 1977. She has translated two screenplays from English to Chinese. They are: *Norman Bethune—The Making of a Hero* (written by Ted Allan, 1980) and *Soong Qingling's Children* (produced and directed by Gary Bush, funded by UNESCO, 1986). Her literary works include *Memoir of Hu Die* (1985), *Dream Chaser* (2008), and *The Forgotten Corner* (2010). She has edited and co-edited over ten literary anthologies in the past ten years. Those anthologies include works from over 170 Chinese writers from all over the world. She was elected as the Chair of Chinese Canadian Writers' Association in 2005 and the Secretary General of Overseas Chinese Women Writers' Association in 2012. She has also been a columnist for three Chinese newspapers published in Canada in the past ten years. She is now a board member of The Society for Chinese Canadian Literature Studies in Vancouver, British Columbia, Canada.

After its first appeareance in a Chinese newspaper, her short story "The Stranger" was republished by the literary magazine *Excellent Literary Works for Appreciation* in China. Later on it was translated into English by Zhu Hong and was published by the *St. Petersburg Review* magazine in New York (2012).

Q & A
WITH LILY LIU

Anna Wang Yuan asked Lily Liu five questions after reading her short story, "The Stranger".

Q: I've heard that you attended the Asian Writers Conference in New Delhi, India, in 1956. That must have been quite an experience, because at that time, very few Chinese writers had the opportunity to communicate with the outside world. Could you tell me more about it?

A: Sixty years ago, as a new graduate from Peking University with a degree in English, I went to the conference with the Chinese delegation as an interpreter. Contrary to your belief, many active writers in China during the 1950s had experience studying or working in Western countries before 1949. The best examples are Lao She, who taught Chinese at the University of London from 1924 to 1929 and Xiao San (aka Emi Siao), who traveled to France for the Work-Study Program in 1920. Many members of the Chinese delegation were fluent in English and/or other foreign languages, and were knowledgeable in foreign literature, which really impressed me. Xiao San was fluent in Russian, French, German, and English. He was very popular at the conference, as was Lao She. After Lao She made his speech, "Writers and Freedom", the conference hall was filled with applause. Even today, I remember that atmosphere clearly. Unfortunately, when the Cultural Revolution broke out in 1966, this elitist group was subject to a cruel purge. When I was writing my story, "The Stranger", I drew inspiration from their fate.

I also met a lot of writers from other countries at the conference. For instance: writers from India—the host country, writers from the Asian republics of the former Soviet Union, and writers from Japan. Japanese writer Yoshi Hotta was the one that I remember most deeply; I learned a lot from the writers all across Asia. Different countries have different cultures, but the value of literature is appreciated across cultures.

Q: Can you describe your work experience at the Institute of Foreign Literature in Chinese Academy of Social Sciences?

A: I majored in English Literature at Peking University and studied a lot of works by 19th century English writers. When I worked at the Institute of Foreign Literature, I also had the chance to study the literary works of Russian writers as well as writers from other countries. Boris Pasternak's *Doctor Zhivago* was banned in the Soviet Union and China in the 1950s. I, however, as a researcher, had access to it, though I did not fully understand the author's intentions at that time. Only about ten years later, when I personally experienced the Cultural Revolution in China, did I realize that *Doctor Zhivago* was about an intellectual's embracement of his dreams and disillusionment. I started creative writing only after I came to Canada. The knowledge of Western literature certainly helped.

Q: Could you describe the writing process of "The Stranger"?

A: The Cultural Revolution in China lasted for ten years and resulted in widespread factional struggles in all walks of life. Millions of people were persecuted across the country and suffered a wide range of abuse including public humiliation, arbitrary imprisonment, torture, and sustained harassment. That ten-year period was a nightmare for most Chinese. I saw and suffered a lot personally as well. I've always wanted to express my experience of this period creatively. Through the characters in "The Stranger", I revealed a small part of how suffering affects a person's beautiful yet heart-wrenching love. Literature in this sense is another way of recording history; it is fictional, yet the environment and characters are drawn from real life. It is united under the author's point-of-view.

Q: Can you talk about your communication with Zhu Hong during the translation of "The Stranger"? I was told that Zhu Hong once asked you, "Who is the stranger in this story, actually?"

A: Good question! Professor Zhu Hong and I both worked at the Institute of Foreign Literature, although she had more seniority. We knew each other during the years of the Cultural Revolution. She is not only a knowledgeable researcher in both English and Chinese, but also a highly skilled translator of literary works, ensuring an accurate translation of a work's emotion and feelings as the author intended.

Yes, she asked me, "Who is the stranger?" Her question caused me to ponder deeply. Sometimes, authors are writing about other people's experiences, but also infuse their own personal experiences and stories as well. In this case, a stranger told her story to another unknown woman. The stranger just wanted to relieve her past and therefore she did not need a response. As for the listener, the stranger's story reminded her of her own experiences. Both of them were strangers to each other and their stories were familiar to all those who lived through the horrors of the Cultural Revolution.

The author's intent is to express the impact of such horror on its victims and hope that such a tragedy is never repeated.

Q: I've heard that once, you met a lady at a fitness club who was reading a copy of *The St. Petersburg Review* and your story, "The Stranger", was in. The lady was very impressed after you told her that you were the author of that story. How did that make you feel?

A: I did not realize that *The St. Petersburg Review* had such a large readership and respected reputation. I felt honored when I found out.

COUNTING DOWN THE MINUTES

by Allan Cho

April 2, 4:53am

Faith Yeung was woken up by a glow of yearning. She yawned and stopped to think about *his* voice.

From her apartment, the landscape over Vancouver's English Bay was still sleepy. It was so quiet that she thought she could hear the rain lightly slap against the raincoats of pre-dawn joggers. Although she enjoyed this same scene every morning for the past twelve years, Faith Yeung felt a new agitation this morning. Things were out of place, the outside was as foreign as the inner workings of her mind. Only eight hours ago, every day had been the same. Now, today stood out and wouldn't roll along as inconspicuously as yesterday or tomorrow.

"Will you miss me?" That was his voice from last night. She closed her eyes, and felt a dash of wetness on her cheeks left by his kisses from last night. Unbeknownst to her until this morning, everything could have shifted, the earth, the sky, and the time.

Faith Yeung realized that she had found what her childhood friends dreamed about and what she never thought was possible: *the one.* She whispered his name, then uttered it aloud, and then screamed only to cover her mouth, fearful of waking her neighbors up. *Peter Shin.*

The last time Faith Yeung's confidence was shaken was only

days ago.

"My dear, as the mother of a beautiful professional who is just turning forty, will I live long enough to see my grandchildren?" Her mother asked in a resplendent Queen's English while the rest of the Yeung clan sipped their oolong tea, their eyes scanning their menus, ears soaking in the drama. Although the restaurant was filled with Cantonese and Mandarin speaking people, Faith Yeung could barely understand the words that were flowing from table to table as smoothly as the aroma of *hargau* (shrimp dumplings) and Shanghainese *xiaolongbao* (steamed dumplings).

Auntie Yee, who acted as Faith's conscience for much of her adult life, interjected, "No matter what you do," she said and took another sip of her tea before continuing, "do not settle." Nestled deep in the woods of her mind, those words of advice carefully guided Faith Yeung as a little girl.

Her mother shot back, "Don't teach my daughter such *nonsense.*" The two continued with their bantering while Faith Yeung coolly fiddled with her Blackberry. Two messages were still left unanswered.

It was difficult to match Auntie Yee's ideal man. After all, her husband had committed treason for love.

"The Yeung family was quite prestigious before 1949, that's why our family didn't think he, a low-ranking army officer, deserved me." As usual, her aunt began the narrative from the first obstacle her husband had fought, "But he never gave up on me until Mother finally relented. We married on the eve of the retreat."[1] It was also the beginning of another tragedy. The Yeung family was deliberately abandoned on the mainland because they were

---

[1] "The retreat" refers to Kuomintang's retreat from mainland China to Taiwan in 1949.

mistrusted by the Kuomintang[2] government.

"He had sailed across the strait along with the army, but when he found out that I was left behind, he immediately turned around and exchanged his life for mine." Auntie Yee sounded sad yet proud. Her husband sold military secrets to Communist China in exchange for the Yeung family to go to North America.

He was later found guilty by a military court and executed.

It was at that time that Faith Yeung once again drew an inevitable conclusion:

No man could possibly compare to him.

But everything is possible, as long as time marches on.

April 14, 3:55am

Faith Yeung laid awake and motionless, her arms carefully folded behind her head. Who would've guessed that despite all the degrees and designations that she had been so diligently collecting, she still felt a nameless void in her life. Not just any man. One who could grow old with her. Not just children either. *Children?* Children meant family, but Faith Yeung had never given much thought about family. It is happiness. It is a natural smile. Is it too late? She unplugged the alarm clock and allowed the room to return to a dark silence.

April 15, 7:01pm

Faith Yeung's father's face lit up when Peter Shin reached out to help him steady his cane. *Good, respect the elder.* The old man thought. Faith Yeung's eyes dashed between Peter Shin and her father while her father's eyes never left Peter Shin's face. Peter Shin stole a fond

---

[2] Kuomintang refers to the political party that governed all or part of mainland China from 1928 to 1949. It is also translated as "The Nationalist" as it appears in Rui Wang's "A Hero of Our Times".

look at Faith Yeung who thought she had even saw a faint redness appear on her father's normally flaccid features. Faith's mother hurried to the door.

"Please come in! What kind of tea do you drink?" Her mother said as she winked at Faith Yeung and silently held her thumb up to the other women as she ushered Peter to the living room. Faith Yeung's heart gradually calmed down. She was nervous about the moment when her parents first met her loved one, but now she realized that the Yeung family would treat every guest in their standard way—tea and dimsum. The only surprise was from Peter Shin. His warm hand reached out for hers, and led her into the room as if it were his territory and she was subject to his powerful leadership, just the way she had imagined since she was a young girl.

"The history of the *pu-erh* tea can be traced back to the Eastern Han Dynasty," Auntie Yee began as she always did to her guests, and then stopped to slowly pour some tea into everyone's cup. "The most famous *pu-erh* tea comes from the Six Famous Tea Mountains of Yunnan. Have you heard of them?"

"Yes, of course, I'm from Menghai," Peter Shin swiveled the cup closer to his nose in order to smell the aroma. Faith was surprised to see that Auntie Yee frowned at Peter Shin, "You're a Mainlander?"

Faith's eyes widened and turned to her aunt. She gripped her cup against her chest.

Peter Shin nodded in silence, and smiled. "As a young boy, I was told that the Tea Mountains were named after six things Zhuge Liang[3] had left behind during the Three Kingdoms." The

---

[3]Zhuge Liang (181–234 C.E.) was a chancellor of the state of Shu Han during the Three Kingdoms period. He is recognized as the greatest and most accomplished strategist of his era, and has been compared to another great ancient Chinese strategist, Sun Tzu. Liang is best known as one of the heroes in *Romance of the Three Kingdoms*.

round table, usually compressed and overtaken by echoing voices of Yeung women, was all of a sudden surrounded by silence beckoning for Peter Shin's soft but insistent words to continue.

"According to the legend, it was he who taught the people of southern Yunnan the art of harvesting and making tea," he continued. The grandfather clock, one of the few objects the Yeung clan had managed to take with them during the Kuomintang withdrawal across the Taiwan Straits, continued to tick for what seemed like hours.

Peter Shin turned to Auntie Yee and continued, "The empire, long divided, must unite; long united, must divide." Auntie Yee pursed her lips and smiled, trying to respond but seemed to struggle for words. Peter Shin patiently broke the silence, "Shall we drink?" The chatter resumed and all was well, perhaps even better.

May 14, 12:30am

Circling Lover's Walk in Stanley Park under the silver moonlight, Faith Yeung and Peter Shin composed poetry, hand-in-hand. Faith Yeung had never found appreciation for words, let alone rhythm. Her mind felt as if it were in the process of laying an egg. "Five, seven, five," Peter Shin told her, "say whatever comes first to your mind." Her chin swiveled towards Peter Shin, and she looked up and into his deep, sunken eyes, a wisp of hair grazed the tip of his brow. A tinge of inspiration.

May 14, 1:45am

Faith Yeung and Peter Shin got up, kissed, and traced some memories onto a bench, in which they returned two days later to further darken with a nail file. In the fine shiny wood they left the loving memory of Alexander and Deborah Goodman. Some words were permanently etched on the park bench, words that continue to fade naturally under the mildew of Vancouver weather, if one looks carefully enough.

Why do feelings grow
Surreptitiously like us
Warmer by the night

June 1, 5:00pm

Faith Yeung had done what was once unthinkable. She took a photograph of herself, and she appeared cheerful.

During a humid afternoon, after an unusual combination of sushi and red wine, Faith Yeung felt dizzy as squares of sunshine shifted melodiously on the large food court walls. Peter Shin helped her into a photo booth. It seemed funny to her that she had to fight to stay still in her pose under the alcohol's influence. It was not until after school when teenagers impatiently lifted the curtains, could Faith Yeung and Peter Shin stop their laughter.

She opened her palms as he put something into it. "Here's yours," he said and continued shearing the miniature photos. They gazed hypnotically at the pair of scissors.

"Is it natural for people my age to do this?" she wondered, almost aloud, only to feel the warmth of Peter Shin smoothing her hair. *What if my colleagues see me? Where would I hide? Have I gone insane?* Peter Shin looked at her, and his frown only triggered more laughter from her. Her body shook, and she felt her ribs aching for breath. For the first time in many years, she felt young again, if only for a brief moment.

Faith looked closely at the pictures. Underneath the pale skin, thinning hair, and crestfallen lips she had been so used to, she was surprised to see what appeared to be a faint resemblance of her past. Her smile, it didn't look anything at all like the forced ones that had accompanied her with each business handshake.

She delighted in an enchantment that seemed to be glowing from her face, almost as a reflection of Peter Shin. Another photo showed her laughing, which looked nothing like the faces she had gotten used to making when she outbid her rivals for a new client. Everything appeared . . . almost genuine. The final photo showed both of them touching lips. When was the last time she felt this way?

June 8, 11:20am

Faith Yeung expected a storm from her family. She expected that many years in the future, she could have a legend of her own to tell the younger generation.

"Our family didn't like the fact that he was from mainland China," she would say, in the same air as Auntie Yee, "but he never gave up on me until Mother finally relented." Or perhaps, she herself could take some credit because she was such a capable mediator.

But strangely, her family kept quiet about her new love affair. No heated discussions. No warnings. No objections. Even Auntie Yee, who used to be so effusive, now clammed up. Faith Yeung was disappointed. As a renowned expert mediator, having lectured at prestigious universities across the world and much sought after on her dispute resolution techniques, she felt helpless when there wasn't a case for her to work on.

She wanted to disappear. One spontaneous afternoon, they drove to San Francisco, taking turns sleeping in the back of the car for fifteen hours until they reached their destination. With Peter Shin, it appeared that time had no purpose and had no point, no beginning and no end. She felt they were like leaves elegantly tracing the paths of wherever the wind wanted them to fall.

"Status of relationship?" the highway patrol officer in reflecting shades asked, clicking his pen and concentrating on his notepad, relieved to know that a speeding ticket would meet his quota for the evening.

"Going well," Peter Shin replied.

The man's eyes followed Peter as he adjusted his seat belt. "Sir, may I ask how you two are related?"

Peter turned to look at Faith, "She's my girlfriend." His hidden words were: *isn't that obvious?*

The officer kept his poker face. "Don't let it happen again," he said as he walked back to his cruiser.

As they continued driving, Faith Yeung couldn't help but wonder: do we look like a couple? She wanted to steal a look at Peter Shin, but somehow she turned away from him. She pressed her head against the window, hands covering her face. They held their silence until Peter Shin stopped along the side of the highway and turned off the ignition. She was surprised.

Peter Shin got out of the car, opened her door and guided her out. They were in the wilderness, facing the patch of highway that connected two states. "I'm not getting any younger," he said, almost in a solemn tone. "This is my last chance." He turned to Faith, and got down on one knee. But far from what Faith hoped it was, it turned out to be the last thing she had expected.

"My company would finance California's 800-mile high-speed rail project. It would start from here," Peter Shin smiled, took her hand, and put it on the pavement in the middle of the highway, as if sharing a secret that only she could know.

Faith felt that Perter seemed to be more of a calculator than a human being. His hand was ice cold. She sneezed and withdrew her hand from his, pretending to cover her nose.

"Excuse me," she said vaguely.

June 14, 3:30pm

The ground beneath Faith shifted again. Peter Shin looked different as she began to examine him more. Was it strange to look at one person so closely and scrutinize every bend and turn without knowing who he really was? Was she seeing him too much? Or not enough? Peter Shin couldn't penetrate Faith's evasiveness. He thought it might have something to do with the lost sense of mystery between them two. He asked Faith to move with him to Shanghai, hoping the imagination for an exotic place could instill vigor to their tired relationship. Faith Yeung shook her head. Shanghai sounded nothing more than a distant version of San Francisco, which they once traveled to escape her family. She didn't believe that running away from her family could give her pleasure anymore.

She slipped back into a deep sleep. In her dream, he turned around and held out his hand, waiting for Faith to catch up.

June 23, 3:30pm

Their first quarrel had the full potential to be the last one. At least, deep down in Faith Yeung's mind, she was fully prepared to break up with Peter after her refusal to move to Shanghai. They had sat serenely through the night at a coffee shop balcony, far above the city, witnessing the fading sunset and vanishing crowd. Peter Shin looked solemn, as if he were at a funeral. Faith Yeung was expecting him to say "goodbye" when his voice broke from the natural composure that she was so accustomed to.

"I can't fathom why anyone could dislike this city," he said, "Can any other place offer us bits and pieces of everywhere? It's the perfect place for us to settle down. "

"To settle down?" Faith Yeung was surprised. "Aren't you going back to Shanghai?"

"I'll stay wherever you choose," Peter Shin said glibly, "Plus, I can still do business in Vancouver. It's a lovely development."

"It rains, it's slow, and you can't really understand what people are saying," she said in haste. "You said you didn't love it here." Secretly, she was annoyed at his use of the word "development" so casually.

"It's a lovely development." Peter Shin repeated the word firmly as if he had the power to decide everything's character. "You'll know what I mean tomorrow."

June 24, 2:04pm

The next morning, Peter Shin took Faith Yeung to May Wah Hotel in Chinatown. Holding an umbrella for her, he wanted to surprise her by showing her his ambitions for a building he could never own. The owners had repeatedly rebuffed his proposals.

"Look, Faith," he pointed to the dilapidated structure, "it can become the gem of this city—high-end luxury nestled in the heart of history."

Peter Shin's voice was slowly drowned out by the sound of raindrops. The languages of her different memories began to float back to Faith Yeung. She remembered the May Wah Hotel as a young girl. It brought back the familiar smells of old Chinatown, like seeping from the back alleys. She had yearned to escape those gluttonous, lazy Sundays strolling down Keefer Street with her grandfather and looking up at old buildings. *Property*, as he called them. She knew them like the back of her hand. They were more than that.

"So what do you think?" he waited, patiently, for a response.

This was the part of the city that Faith Yeung had been avoiding. She identified as a Chinese Canadian, not Chinatown Chinese. Those were different. Most of the generation which she had grown up with had moved, either to other parts of Canada, or back to Asia. As a well-educated, capable professional, she chose to settle down at English Bay, a prestigious sea-side residential area ten kilometers away from Chinatown. But no matter how she felt about old Chinatown, in the back of her mind, she still thought it was hers. She felt offended when she listened to Peter Shin's grand plan of tearing the May Wah Hotel down and building a wholly new property on the land. *Property.* She felt the word was disgusting.

"My grandfather built Shanghai from the ground up." Peter Shin smiled, his left brow gestured with confidence. "I'm going to do the same over here." He smiled, and received no response.

"Faith," Peter made his final proposal, "I want you to help me build this empire."

Faith Yeung wondered why Peter's passionate pleas sounded so flawed and hollow in her ears. What went wrong between them? She smiled and curled her fingers around his. His fingers lost the warmth she felt months ago when they strolled under the moonlight. Suddenly, it occurred to her: that was the coldness of new money.

July 16, approximately 4:33pm

This world that they had discovered together seemed to dissolve, first slowly, then all at once.

Faith Yeung watched Peter Shin walk up to her, a cup of iced chai latte in one hand and Faith Yeung's favorite kind of brownie in the other. Brownies were a dessert that she could never wean from her diet, regardless of how much she had wanted to.

This scene looked so mundane to Faith Yeung, so different compared to the great love Auntie Yee experienced. Why couldn't she love him anymore in spite of their differences, even though

61

Auntie Yee and her husband could?

Peter Shin wove through the crowd and walked up to Faith Yeung, who was sitting at a table in the dining area at Vancouver International Airport, a carry-on bag sitting beside her. She smiled at Peter, but her smile looked blank.

They sat down to gossip about the little daily things that all couples talk about at their usual table while being serenaded by the scales of Mozart's Requiem. However, she couldn't distinguish his voice. The cloak had been lifted, she could see more clearly now. She saw a tired man before her. The slippery silver hair, torrents of wrinkles, the hunched shoulders, and the forced small talk. The audacious, romantic Peter Shin had never existed but in her mind. She had fabricated love, it was never there, and now she was on the verge of regret.

"When are you coming back?"

"It could be months. You know, those Arabian customers could be very difficult." Faith Yeung tried her best to sound nice, but she surprised herself at how her voice turned cold.

"I can't live without you," Peter said, genuinely, "I want you to travel with me."

"Does it always have to be *us*?" she said in her mind. But instead, she blurted out, "You'll be fine."

"No!" Peter grabbed Faith's hand.

Faith's hand twitched. She tried her best not to withdraw it from Peter's grasp. However, her neck tingled uncomfortably. *He is a stranger*. She thought. How random, how impulsive, and how childish this all seemed, that she could conceivably throw herself —all that she's built up for the past years—at this peculiar person who she had actually wanted to hold on to physically and spiritually only three months ago.

She understood herself more clearly than before. She remembered her refusal to work anywhere else for months after her rejection by Ernst & Young; she reapplied four times until she was accepted. If she wanted the best, she couldn't settle for second. Love was a game for her too. If she couldn't achieve the most romantic, obtain the most superior love affair, how could she possibly justify stooping down to marry a heap of money?

This was not solely about her, but rather her against the absurdity of life's games, of its unwritten rules. Quickly and subtly, her logic floated to the surface. Her mind achieved clarity again, almost relief.

"What are you thinking, dear?" Peter Shin's voice interrupted.

The creases of her smile deepened, and she made no immediate reply.

July 17, 8:33pm

Faith Yeung left Vancouver International Airport. The first thing she did was go to a Fido retailer to change one of her phone numbers. She had two mobile numbers, one for business and the other for personal use. After that, she went back home.

Faith Yeung tossed herself onto her bed and felt tears soaking through her pillow, even though she did not cry. This vacant feeling of freedom suddenly seemed foreign to her again. She hated feeling it again. She hated the scathing irony of how fragile and taciturn human emotions can be, how one moment she could tear herself to bits and pieces for one person, only to turn to steel and cold iron the very next.

She got up, unplugged her clock radio, and threw it across the room, leaving a deep scar on the wall. Everything was dark again. She fell asleep shortly after, dreaming of nothing.

July 18, 5:00am

Just before she left for her morning meeting, Faith Yeung walked up to her window with a cup of warm coffee in her hands, and peered out at the familiar landscape. She did not feel happiness, nor sadness. Was it indifference? She didn't have time to think; she was already late for a meeting with her client. But just as she was about to turn away, she caught a blue streak of remaining snow on the mountain, and hanging yarns of clouds spread gently across the sky. She felt words slipping autonomously from her mouth.

Can emptiness fill
And capture a mind, a heart?
We don't know, don't care.

ABOUT THE AUTHOR

ALLAN CHO is a writer based in Vancouver, Canada, and a librarian at the University of British Columbia. His works has been published in multiple literary and arts magazines, including *Ricepaper Magazine*, *Georgia Straight*, and *Diverse Magazine*. He volunteers for a number of community causes in Canada, including organizing literASIAN, the very first Asian Canadian writers' festival.

Allan Cho at LiterASIAN Writers Festival 2015

Allan Cho with Korean Canadian poet Bong Ja Ahn

Q & A
WITH ALLAN CHO

Anna Wang Yuan asked Allan Cho five questions after reading his story, "Counting Down the Minutes".

Q: Please tell me more about your writing. For instance, do you write on a daily basis?

A: I'm constantly writing, sometimes on paper, often in my mind. I tend to jot down ideas and piece them back together later. I'm working on several short stories and book projects at the moment. I've been working on this story, "Counting Down the Minutes", for over five years, and it has evolved over those years. The characters, tone, setting, and dialogue very much changed during this time. I like letting the characters play out in my mind like actual human beings, and I like watching them grow and mature.

Q: Your story is like the antithesis of the story of *Romeo and Juliet*. Faith and Peter are from different sides of the Taiwan Strait, but the differences only generate mutual interests for a brief moment, at least that's the case for Faith. Is there any message you tried to get across here?

A: I was not interested in writing a love story. This story is an evolution of a love affair from beginning to end, and part of writing it is a reflection of so many underdeveloped relationships that have so much promise but never go anywhere. Typical love stories in popular culture tend to highlight and idealize romantic relationships. I'm more interested in the numerous relationships that don't work out, the ones that we as a society tend to dismiss and sweep under the rug like a stray strand of hair. But I think there's much more to a dying relationship that we must first understand before we can move on.

Q: Who are your favorite writer(s)? Who do you think influenced you the most?

A: My reading interests vary and are eclectic, spanning the genres and cultures. There's a number of writers who have influenced me, including Chuck Palahniuk, F. Scott Fitzgerald, Michael Lewis, and Eileen Chang. But Michael Ondaajte really helped build my early foundation as a writer, as I would re-read and copy certain passages by hand to absorb the author's elegant and poetic style.

Q: Every writer in this anthology except you were asked whether they felt comfortable writing in English. You are the only writer in this anthology whose first language is English. I guess that question doesn't apply to you. Still, is there anything you can tell me about your relationship with any language, be it English or Chinese?

A: Although I write in English, my stories tend to deal with non-Western characters and themes. The dialogue is usually in another language. In "Counting Down the Minutes", I oftentimes struggle with writing the dialogue in English after translating from Chinese (Cantonese & Mandarin). I think this duality is critical in making the story flow well, so I put in double the amount of effort to actually imagine the situations and exchanges in the original language. Doing this language "switch" is hugely rewarding but extremely time consuming.

Q: If you could choose freely, which country would you prefer to live in?

A: I've stayed in numerous cities, and while I've enjoyed them, I still love Vancouver (Canada) the most. There's a love-hate relationship with this city among Vancouverites. Did you know that it's one of the most expensive cities to live in? Growing up in Vancouver, I've often heard people complain about its banality; those who were born here usually left for bigger places like Hong Kong or Toronto. There was a time when those who stayed behind didn't do so because of choice, but because of family. But things have changed recently. People begrudgingly acknowledge the power and draw of Vancouver brought about by the new immigrants. People now get to know Vancouver through shows like "Real Housewives of Vancouver". I liken it to seeing a modest supporting actor become an overnight A-list celebrity movie star. While at the same time, it's skyrocketed to the world index of most expensive real estate glory (or infamy). With new fame comes new friends, new experiences, and the allure of many new distractions. So, it's at a crossroad: how should the city handle its new found wealth and status? How should it go about in life? What's next? I want to see how this city evolves, and I want to be a part of it. This feeling, as well as the tension and cultural differences between those born here and those who have recently arrived, inspired me to write "Counting Down the Minutes".

THE
STRANGERS

PART 2

"I'm a stranger in a strange land."

— **Carson McCullers**
The Heart Is A Lonely Hunter

THE BUG

by Lily Chu

I knew almost nothing about it, except that it originally came from Pakistan. I didn't know its shape and size, its likes and dislikes, or whether it ever had any fears or dreams—an enigma, indeed, it seemed.

Well, let us start from the very beginning—in Pakistan.

The contract we signed in order to work for the Asian Bank in Pakistan contained a shipment clause which stated that we were entitled to a three-and-a-half ton cargo space for furniture and personal effects. To both of us who were used to traveling light, this seemed to be an unnecessary waste.

We enjoyed ethnic colors and flavors wherever we went, and would prefer to use native arts and crafts for our house decorations if we were to live in that country. We really could not think of any furniture and personal effects that we could not live without. Why did we have to incur such exorbitant costs, although not from our pocket, in order to ship our things across the ocean? We therefore used this allowance for all the academic books we could collect, and then donated them to a Pakistani university in Islamabad upon our arrival. One year later, our work was done and we were ready to return to the States. We once again found this three-and-half ton of shipping allotment waiting for us. By this time, we had purchased several intricately hand-made Pakistani carpets, which were beautiful beyond compare. Of course, we had to ship them home with us. Since these carpets were not enough to fill up the cargo space, we wanted to think of something else to include. One day, we happened upon a marble shop at the local market. There were marble slabs of various colors, from green to white, and red to black, all with interesting grains and patterns, and we quickly lost our heads right then and there. Before we knew what we were doing, we became the new owners of twelve boxes of pink marble that came from the quarry in Quetta, a place in Baluchistan, south of the Afghan border. Now, we thought, since we were crazy enough to buy these heavy boxes of marble to ship across the globe, we might as well go all the way and get some wood which we had always coveted.

The market was a bustling place filled with loud noises, honking cars, crowds of people, and small shops on both sides of the alley with goods spilled out onto the pavement. It was distinctly lacking women; only a few figures covered with black burqas from head to toe floated in and out of the market like ghosts. Not far from the marble shop in the market stood a wood shop. The stall was dark and small, with a few wood planks of different lengths leaning against the wall. The wood *wallah* (seller), an old man who wore a turban on his head and had an impressive big beard, told us that he could order any type of wood for us, as his warehouse was really the forest in the faraway mountains. He became visibly frustrated with us and thought we were crazy because we wanted to buy wood, but wouldn't allow him to order a tree from the forest to be cut down. He thought for a long time, during which we drank obligatory tea and exchanged obligatory pleasantries, and the old man told us about this ancient Shisham tree. The log from this tree had been dried under the sun in the village for quite some time now; however, nobody wanted to buy it because a part of it showed signs of wood borer infestation. He told us that Shisham was a slow growing rosewood tree from northern India and Pakistan and its hard, dense, red hued wood had been highly treasured for fine furniture making throughout the centuries. If we would like to buy it, this *wallah* said, he could order it to be cut into thick planks.

However, he carefully added, as an ethical and reputable *wallah* would, that he could not guarantee that the planks would be completely free from wood borers, even though the log had been dried for a long time now and would be treated with insecticide before it was sold to us. If we shipped these planks all the way to the States and found borers in them, that would be regrettable.

We thought this *wallah* was so unusually honest that it was truly remarkable. We did not really mind if the wood we bought had been eaten by some borers. Now, with his words of caution, we began to worry if the borers we inadvertently transported into the States would eat up our national forests and lead to a major environmental disaster.

It was amazing how one single log could be cut into twenty-five long planks, and it was even more amazing how heavy these planks turned out to be. They were shipped by a truck to the Custom and Transportation Division. Soon afterwards, a gentleman from the Custom Division came to visit and told us in no uncertain words that these planks were too heavy and bulky to be contained in the three-and-a-half ton container. We invited him inside our house and served him obligatory tea, and Harold spoke obligatory pleasantries to him in his native Urdu language, which obviously made a big impression. Harold asked him what kind of material the container was made of, and the gentleman said it was pine board. Harold asked him if we could build our own container using our Shisham planks instead of pine board. He stuttered for a while and said that nobody in his right mind would use such good wood for a container since the wood would be scratched and ruined during the transportation. We said that was alright with us. He continued to protest and said that the Shisham wood was very hard and would take a lot of work to be made into a container. Harold took out a hundred-rupee bill and asked, "Would this compensate for your extra work?" The poor fellow looked at the bill and could fight no more.

To our friends in the States, however, we *were* amazing people for transporting stones and wood from abroad. We eventually used the pink marble for the fireplace in our Sandcastle, an adobe house we built ourselves in southern New Mexico. When we sat in front of the dancing flames, the pink marble greeted us, its grains forming patterns and pictures reminiscent of the Himalaya Mountains and Punjabi plains. The Shisham wood, on the other hand, stayed in storage after my Harold applied a good amount of borer-killing solution to them. We found the sheer volume and the heavy weight of these planks simply daunting and did not know what to do with them.

Once in a while, some wood-loving friends would come to visit, and we would then take them to the storage shed to show off a bit. No one had ever seen this kind of wood; they would inevitably marvel at the sight of this dark-red rosewood, touching its interesting patterns and grains, and commenting that only walnut would have such unusually dark and hard texture.

We were happy to share our loot with friends; all our wood-loving friends carried some of the planks home, while the rest stayed in storage, gathering dust. There they stayed, for three long years.

My husband Harold said one day, "Should we do something with these rosewood planks? What a shame to let them just rot away in storage? What in the world can we possibly do with them?"

After much discussion, we finally decided to use the planks as panels for our bedroom wall.

Actually, we knew it was sacrilegious to use such rare rosewood as wall paneling. However, we did not have the skills required to make furniture.

Even the simple task of applying them to the wall turned out to be much more demanding than we anticipated. To start with, Pakistani carpenters obviously believed that the principle of wood cutting was to make as many planks out of a log as possible, and as such, every single plank had a different size, length, and thickness. Furthermore, this old rosewood had been dried for such a long time that it had somehow morphed into iron, or so it seemed to us. None of our woodworking machines or tools could cut it, and we had to ship it to a specialty shop to make them more or less the same thickness and much smoother. When we got the planks back from the shop and tried to nail them on the wall with a hammer, every single nail inevitably bent. We finally had to drill holes into the planks with an electric drill, and only then were we able to use a hammer and nails. The process was so slow, and the planks were so irregular in shape and size, that we felt like we were putting up a jigsaw puzzle on the wall. However, the finished product was simply stunning beyond anyone's imagination. Rustic and yet elegant, the wall was now adorned with swirling coils of the growth rings, a marvelous abstract painting. The light yellow marks left by the wood borers were highlights in the dark red grain. It was reminiscent of floating lights on a pond and drifting clouds in the sky.

I often gazed at the finished wood panels, and tried hard to imagine the ancient Shisham tree it once was. What was it like, when it stood exuberantly with all its glory under the hot Pakistani sun? Did it hold many bird nests in the arm of its branches? Did it provide shade for the townsfolk that walked by? How much of the sky had its branches grasped as they soared upward? Its leaves, were they long or round; were they small and lined-up like feathers? When spring arrived in Pakistan, what kind of flowers did it put forth? Did these flowers fall to the ground and carpet the street? Did they fall on the backs of donkeys as they walked by with tinkling bells around their necks? During evenings in the depth of autumn, did this tree immerse itself in the silvery moonlight and listen to the sighs of its falling leaves?

Life has this amazing ability to make us numb to anything that has been with us for a while. Under the mounting pressure of a busy life, with so many matters competing for my attention, I eventually started to look at the wall without really seeing it.

Life is like that. It is notorious for making us run around in circles like a rodent in a hamster wheel, without knowing what we are doing. Life is really this massive grinding stone with rough edges that bit by bit, piece by piece, every minute and every hour, relentlessly grinds us down. We slowly change into distorted shapes, with weight gained, bodies stooped over, and wrinkles all over our faces. Our dreams gradually dim, fade, and become distant. Eventually you don't even recognize yourself any more.

But life must go on.

When was this? Which particular night was this? In the silent depth of the midnight stillness, I suddenly heard a sound—

It was a very faint sound, trembling humbly, as it appeared to come and go, sometimes close and sometimes far away. It was as if it could only be heard in the dead of night when the whole world became absolutely silent, and when you tuned your antennae to a certain frequency or wavelength and listened with all your might then you would be able to hear this rhythmic z . . . z . . .

z . . . z . . .z . . .

I suspected that I might have a ringing in my ear. Then, I started to wonder if an electronic device, such as the alarm clock or the telephone next to my bed, had emitted some high pitched sound.

I woke up Harold. Half asleep, he listened for a while and pronounced that I had a rich imagination.

I disconnected the alarm clock and the telephone. However, the mysterious sound persisted, as if it were a sound inside my head and only I could hear it.

I could not figure out where the sound had come from, and the more I thought about it, the more puzzled and frustrated I became.

It was quite some time later before Harold also heard the sound. He was just as mystified; he got up in the middle of the night, gently touching this and probing that, all the while straining his ears to listen intently in all directions. All of a sudden, he burst out laughing and declared that we now had an illegal immigrant in our midst.

Harold said it could be wood borers that we imported from Pakistan. It might also be eggs laid by the wood borers, and now they had hatched into bugs. The sound we heard was the noise they made while chewing the wood.

Instantly, my hair stood on end. The panels that my head touched every night had bugs chewing in them! Who knew when they would get out and became illegal immigrants in my bed?

Harold tried to calm me down and said that he only heard one bug. He explained that this kind of bug grew extremely slow, and it might take a long time before it would get out of the wood panel. Besides, he reasoned logically, even if it escaped, there were two probabilities. The possibility that it would escape out of our side of the panel to reach our bed was only one in two.

Citing unbiased statistics made Harold sound almost scientific. However, it did not pacify me at all. I could only think about this unseen bug, which for all I knew might have been well equipped with six hairy legs and an ugly proboscis. Right at this moment, it was chewing the hard wood next to my bed and could come over uninvited anytime.

For my sake, Harold bought extra strength bug killer from Home Depot. He put on a major show of spraying and splashing; he even dug holes into the panels with electric drills and injected the killer solution inside. All these activities turned our bedroom into a battle ground; smoke in the room obscured our vision. An awful smell lingered and made breathing impossible. If the solution wouldn't kill the bug, it certainly would kill me. I picked up my pillows and moved to the couch in the sunken living room so I could sleep.

Two weeks later, when I returned to our bed, I heard the same faint sound—z . . . z . . . z . . . z . . . .z . . .

In the dead of night, when even thoughts and feelings were frozen in the dark shadows, only this creature from another country deeply buried inside the wood was relentlessly boring away and making the rhythmic noise—z . . . z . . . z . . . z . . .z . . .

Every single "z" was the sound of it chomping a mouthful of wood. As it chewed its way forward, it created a narrow passageway, barely wide enough for it to wiggle ahead, but not enough room for it to turn around and back out either. How could it live in such confinement, never seeing the light of day? How could it possibly survive by eating such dry and hard wood? But if you could stop and think for a moment, if you were born as a wood bug, what could you possibly do apart from eating wood as you bored a tunnel through it?

It was just that I couldn't help but think about it. Deeply buried inside this hard as iron slab of wood, living, breathing, wriggling, and emitting its faint calls, was a bug.

However, *in the depth of the night and in a foreign land that had no other creature of your kind*, I said to the bug, *who could hear you? and who could understand your cries?*

Ah! The dark night was so lonely, so bottomlessly deep. In our mundane existence of muddling along in this world, squeezed among the bustling crowds and toiling to make a living, buried deeply in everyone's heart is a cry, waiting to be heard, waiting for someone to understand.

I was reminded of Lord Byron's poem, where the prisoner is chained to a stone pillar, deep in a living grave, below the surface of the lake in the Castle of Chillon. I could almost visualize him, going through years without hearing a sound or seeing a face, ceaselessly tapping the stone wall in his dungeon, his heart silently crying, "I am here! Can anyone hear me?"

But we usually don't utter a sound, and we only hear the dead silence of the deserted valley.

Once in ancient China, the bell from the Cold Mountain Temple tolled at midnight and its sound drifted through the dark and frosty night into the ears of a traveler who happened to be moored by the Maple Bridge. Instantly, the sound stirred in his melancholic heart and poured out as a beautiful poem, *Mooring at Night by the Maple Bridge*. At the Xun-Yan River harbor, in a bygone era in ancient China, the sound of the Pipa instrument passed through maple leaves and reed flowers in the autumn crispness of the evening to reach a lonely poet. The music brought tears to the Chiang-Zhou magistrate, which soaked the poet's long blue robe.

In the total stillness of the surrounding darkness, when a sound from the outside finally reaches us, is it merely that sound we are hearing? Or are we hearing its echoes reverberating in the deserted valleys of our own hearts?

Life continued to put pressure on me and my schedule became busier by the day—tenure, promotion, publication, meetings, conferences, professional registration, and practice certification. A gentleman also invited me to start a business with him. Every task had the magical power to multiply into one hundred tasks. I traveled to South America, Central America, China, and Africa to consult. There were endless meetings to attend and new projects waiting to be done. Work kept piling up, new things on top of the old, until I could no longer find anything. The article I wanted to write was not written, the letter I needed to reply to did not receive a response, the book I wanted to read did not get read, and the photos I wanted to develop remained in the camera.

Life was like a streetcar named desire speeding ahead of me. I tried desperately to catch it. However, it forever stayed ahead of me, seemingly within my reach if I could only try a bit harder. With the elusive distance of just a few inches, I tried with all my heart, but could never quite get to it.

As we grew older, the days passed by even faster. Time also seemed to take delight in galloping ahead, from minutes to hours, from hours to days, from days to months, from months to years, and many, many years before we even knew it.

Occasionally, I woke up in the middle of the night and could still hear the sound of the bug, so I knew it was still there, still munching away at the wood, boring its tunnel. The creature was still the same creature, and its life remained the same life. Such was our lot! Just like that!

At work, meetings seemed to be the staple of life. There were meetings after meetings, all day long. There were even special meetings just to organize all other meetings. Once, everybody at the meeting argued till we were all red in the face. Someone even jumped up on the conference table. We were all convinced that if our suggestions were not adopted, the college would face dire consequences and would simply cease to exist. The scheduled time to end the meeting had long passed, but nobody was willing to give in. Their voices became louder and louder, as if a war were about to break out at any moment.

Suddenly, I laughed aloud. Everybody was startled and looked at me as if I had lost my mind.

I couldn't explain it to them. We are actually all bugs, creatures cloistered in our own dry and hard wood. We believe our world inside this wood is the entire universe, and we think that other people should be just like us and be willing to eat the same dry wood and wiggle their way through the same narrow tunnel.

If you are a bug and you do not know you are a bug, then that's alright. Anyway, that's what the life of a bug is like—not so good, but not that bad either. Life is just like that after all.

However, if you are a bug and you know you are a bug, then what? How would you live? How can you live on?

I began to lose sleep. Knowing that you are a bug is truly painful and unsettling; no wonder people prefer not to know.

That night, when the world seemed dead, I lay on my bed and tried to adjust to a wavelength that I had not tuned in to for some time. I listened attentively for what seemed like forever and heard nothing.

Only after a long while, there appeared a weak z . . . z . . .

I realized that this bug was about to die.

I used the digits on both my hands to count and decided that this bug probably had lived inside this wood for about ten years. I never thought it possible that a wood borer could live in the wood for such a long time; obviously, it was about time for it to pass away at this ripe, old age.

We always assume that we will stay young forever and that time is on our side. We know full well that all creatures that are ever born will eventually die, but we cannot comprehend when death will strike. Everything we have, we take for granted, as if it is ours due to our inalienable rights, and nothing could snatch it away from us. What we don't have, regardless of cost, we grab it, we fight for it, we pile it up, we build it.

Haven't you seen those grandiose pyramids built by the pharaohs in ancient Egypt with the sweat and toil of countless slaves? Nothing could prevent them from crumbling and collapsing eventually into the desert sands.

Honestly, only gravity and time will last and remain as the winners.

I submitted my resignation letter to my boss. He was shocked and asked me what had happened.

I said that there wasn't anything wrong. I just wanted to do things that I've never had the chance to do.

He wanted to know if I wanted a raise or a promotion. He said that I was the only person in the office that both sides would listen to.

I smiled and said that was nice of him to say. I told him that I would like to leave while everybody still had such good will toward me.

Thus, I changed my work schedule from full-time to part-time, teaching only one course a week, and I did not have to attend meetings at all.

THE BUG

Once the decision was made, I found out it wasn't actually so difficult. Walking out of my boss's office, right away I felt as if a load had been lifted from my shoulders. By the time I left the school building, I began to notice the brilliant sunshine on this early summer day and the seemingly endless expanse of the desert sky.

When I returned to our house in the country, I found out, to my surprise, that our pecan trees had grown lush and shady. A pack of squirrels with puffy tails and big eyes lived near the irrigation ditches. They were running in and out of water pipes in the ground. When they caught sight of me, they showed no sign of fear, as if they were the real owners of the farm.

In the pond, which sat in front of our abode, there were wild ducks and cranes that had made their homes. From time to time, we could see Canadian geese, blue herons, and an occasional stray seagull. Recently, the jujubes behind our house had ripened. From nowhere came a family of four red foxes, a mommy and her three young babies, who obviously decided to stay to take advantage of the sweet red dates. I often hid inside the house and watched the babies stand on their hind legs while they reached out to steal our jujubes.

The newly developed lily pond on the southern side of the house was filled with koi fish and planted with lotus. This was the first summer that the flowers bloomed; the petals were deep red in the beginning, but bleached by the brilliant sun they slowly turned into a soft pink. While I had not been paying attention, the lotus flowers had presented to us the exotic smile of the faraway land.

And the bug really had died. Harold and I listened carefully and heard nothing. We looked up and down the wood, searching with a flashlight, but we never found any wood traces or boreholes that might have been created by the bug.

So, the bug finally had died. It was born in the wood, lived in the wood, and died in the wood. It ate nothing but the wood, lived in holes dug out of the wood, and never saw one ray of sunshine or a single patch of the blue sky.

I whole-heartedly wished that it never knew it was a bug.

LILY CHU has a Ph.D. in Educational Psychology. She is a Certified Medical Technologist and a Counseling Psychologist as well. She has taught at Lake Superior State University and New Mexico State University for a total of 30 years. Besides university teaching, research, and administration, she has served in many developing countries as a consultant. Chinese creative writing has been an unexpected joy and accomplishment in her life. She has published six books in Chinese and has two more books forthcoming. While working as a professor, Lily Chu published approximately forty research articles and professional monograms in English. Recently, she has been a regular contributing author to an English magazine, *Friends of We Chinese in America*, which features essays and fiction. She will be participating in the "14th International Conference on the Short Story in English." Her short story, "Fairy Mother", will be included in their Short Story Anthology. Lily Chu was the Director of the National Education Association Grant on "Minorities and Women in Educational Research." She is the President of the San Diego Chinese Writers' Association and will be the President of Overseas Chinese Women Writers' Association in 2016.

Lily Chu delivering a speech at a conference hosted by the Southern U.S. Chinese Writers' Association in 2015

Q & A
WITH LILY CHU

Anna Wang Yuan asked Lily Chu six questions after reading her story, "The Bug".

Q: I understand that your story "The Bug" is based on a real story that happened in your life. How much of the story is drawn from real events and why can it be called fiction?

A: This story is 100% factual. We shipped some old wood boards from Pakistan and made bedroom wall panels out of them. A faint noise at night baffled us, and after a careful investigation, we determined that we had an illegal immigrant hidden in the wall panels. This bug lived in that hard wood, ate the wood, breathed in the wood, and eventually died in the wood. It made me think what kind of life, what kind of existence, and what a terrible waste that was. I eventually came to the realization that it did not differ from the lives most of us live. I think there are two reasons why it can be called fiction. First, the true story sounds like a fabrication. Think about it, a bug hid in a wood plank, traveled from Southeast Asia to America, and finally died in a foreign country. It is not something that would happen every day, isn't it? Second, I put in a lot of my own emotion and imagination in it. I think that mapping out the events and digging deeply into my own thoughts is the process of creative writing.

Q & A

Q: Let me quote a sentence from your story "The Bug": "We enjoyed ethnic colors and flavors wherever we went, and would prefer to use native arts and crafts in our house decoration if we were to live in that country." Can you share more experiences like that with me?

A: I have written a book called, *Golden Spider-web: Walking in the African Jungle*. As the title infers, it is about my travels in Africa. As I walked in the Zimbabwe jungle, I came across, by accident, enormous crocheted tablecloths that were hanging from the trees and were for sale. They turned golden by the setting sun and reminded me of a web of interconnection between people. At that moment, I suddenly had the title for my future book. Of course, the book is more than that. While I was traveling in Africa, I was shaken by the primitive and throbbing life forces and was touched by the gentle human connections that occur every day.

Q: You seem to have traveled extensively. What other countries have you traveled to?

A: My husband and I have traveled widely, including some very rural and isolated corners of the world. Our travels are mostly work-related. Both of us have served in developing countries as consultants. When I talk about traveling, I'm not talking about flying to a foreign country, staying there for a week or two and then flying back home. My husband and I actually had a life there. We have lived, as well as worked, in Pakistan, Namibia, Swaziland, and Belize. We chose this life. My husband is an internationalist.

Q: If you could choose freely, which country would you prefer to live in?

A: Firstly, I don't think we are ever "free" to choose where we live. They are so many factors which are beyond our control and they dictate our choices. I am in the process of finishing a Chinese book entitled *Home Is Nowhere and Everywhere*. The title of this book pretty much reflects my philosophy. I will make a home wherever I find myself in, while I really don't have a home in this world. To answer your question directly, I will live in any country where I happen to find myself.

Q: Please tell me more about your writing. What language do you find more comfortable to use when you're writing?

A: My academic training is in Educational Psychology. Therefore, for many years, I wrote academic and scientific papers in English. I was rather at ease with English technical writing, however, it is rather hard for me to switch to creative writing in English, as I do creative writing mainly in Chinese. I have published eight Chinese books, mainly collections of short stories. I have only started to write short stories in English recently. I would like to write more short stories in English if I can find publication sources. I do find the need to introduce Chinese writers, with their unique perspectives, to English readers.

Q: Can you name your favorite English writer(s)? I found that your stories were filled with symbolism and metaphors. Is there a particular writer, like Kafka, who has influenced you?

A: I knew you would ask me about Kafka! No. My story, "The Bug", often reminds readers of the varmint in Kafka's famous book, *The Metamorphoses*. But the similarity ends there. While Kafka wrote about alienation, guilt, and absurdity in his story, my story points to hope, choice, and breakthrough, I think.

Yet, I do like Kafka's books. His statements, "Many a book is like a key to unknown chambers within the castle of one's own life" and "A book must be the axe for the frozen sea within us" echo in my heart. He also said that his works were all about his father, and that rings true for me also. Come to think about it, I guess Kafka did influence me.

Actually, my favorite author is Kuzuo Ishiguro. I identify with his straddling between two distinctively different cultures, and I admire his extraordinary writing prowess. There is a dreamy quality in his writing where time and space are fluid, reality and impressions become fleeting and interchangeable. When you gaze deeply into the characters in his novels, you seem to look into the negative of a photo. I am often mesmerized by his stories.

THE HOUSE IN AVENEL

by Jieru Zhou
Translated by Ying Alexandra Cao

A little bear and a little tiger lived in a little house; they were best friends. One day they found a crate of bananas in the river; it came from Panama. They decided to go to Panama, the land of their dreams. They met many animals on their way, a fox and a crow, a hedgehog and a hare. When the little bear and the little tiger asked for the way to Panama, all the animals told them to turn left. If you keep on turning left, where would you end up? Yes, quite correct. Finally, the little bear and the little tiger had returned to their home. As time went by, their house was rather weather beaten, so they couldn't recognize it. But they were very happy; they thought this place was the land of their dreams, Panama.[1]

I often dreamed about the house I used to live in when I was in China. I dreamed about its front and back door. I saw my green mailbox and I opened it again and again. I discovered outdated newspapers and magazines, all soaked by rain or snow. When I was twenty, I left that house and moved to California. Within California, I moved several times. I moved a lot after leaving California until I finally settled down in Avenel, New Jersey. Right after I

---

[1] This paragraph is the synopsis of Janosch's famous children's book, *The Trip to Panama*. Janosch (born March 11, 1931) is one of the best-known German artists and children's book authors. The author of this story retold Janosch's story after she read a Chinese translation of *The Trip to Panama*.

crammed my old furniture inside my new house in Avenel, I started dreaming about the place where I was born and raised. I never
dreamed about any of the other houses.

You think they might just as well have stayed home all this time; you think
they didn't need to take a trip to Panama at all.

You are wrong.

Because then they would never have met the fox and the crow, they would
never have met the hedgehog and the hare, and they would never have realized
how comfortable a homey, soft, plushy sofa could be.

Avenel was full of Indian and Pakistani people. If someone wanted
to be close to fellow Chinese people, Avenel was not the place. But
I went out to the world to meet a fox, a crow, a hedgehog, and a
hare. I met Anita and May in Avenel. Anita was Polish and May
was Indonesian. They lived among foreigners so they were used to
speaking English.

Anita was the kind of person you could hit off with instantly.
The first time we met, she told me that her husband was twenty
years older than her. I felt like she told me this information way too
soon, and I didn't know how to respond. I made a funny face and
gave her a compliment. I think I said that an older man was more
likely to be wiser and know how to love someone better.

I remember that Anita winked at me.

May had two kids, aged one and three. Every morning at sev-
en, she put her two children in the car, strapped them in their car
seats, and drove her husband to the train station. In the afternoon,
when the kids took a nap, she went outside to her small yard and
did chores. I passed by one day while she was washing her car. We
greeted each other.

"Have a cup of tea with me," she said. "These cookies are best
with tea." It turned out that she was selling homemade cookies.

"Ten dollars for a huge jar." She made an exaggerated expression, "delicious and it's a good price."

She was wearing a loose frock, probably without a bra underneath. Her hair was dry and frizzy. She obviously didn't take care of herself. Her house was clean and neat, though. The windows were so clean that I barely noticed their existence. The sofa was white, soft, and plushy. The car parked in the short drive way was white, too. It's hard to keep everything white when you have two kids.

And then they mended their house. Everything was just as good as it used to be. The little bear went fishing and the little tiger went looking for mushrooms. In fact, it was even better than it used to be because they bought themselves a soft, plushy sofa. They thought their little house amongst the bushes was the most beautiful place in the whole world. "Panama is the land of our dreams, and we can stay here forever and ever."

I paid for the jar of cookies. They were really good.

If I had to choose whether to speak to Anita or May, I would choose May. Anita made me nervous, while May was more level-headed.

May took afternoon breaks between her various outdoor jobs. She sometimes ventured to my house to use the fax machine or printer. "I'll pay you," she said. May kept her promise. She printed out coupons and used my fax machine to send handwritten documents. I was a bit curious about what was written on the papers, but I never acted upon my curiosity. May carefully placed the papers face-down every time. *Whatever.* I thought to myself. *As long as she pays for the long-distant telephone fees.*

May called me one afternoon and asked if she could use the fax machine as usual. After she was done sending a fax, May asked me if she could use my computer. "Just five minutes," she said.

I said it was okay and then left her alone. Five minutes turned into a hundred minutes, and she was still hunched over at my desk. I had to intervene and walked up behind her. I caught her chatting with someone online.

"I have to tell you the truth," May said sheepishly, "my husband is home today."

"Doesn't he allow you to use the computer?" I said.

"Yes and no. Please don't look at me that way. I was talking with my ex-boyfriend. I was supposed to marry him, but I married my husband instead. That was a mistake because my husband is an asshole."

"Why do you say that?" I asked. May's husband was a computer engineer. He spoke English well and didn't have an accent. I only spoke with him once or twice. He looked like a decent man.

"My husband slept with his secretary." May was on the verge of tears.

"Well," I shrugged and politely said that I needed to use my computer. May looked disappointed and left.

If I had allowed May to continue, she would have gone on and on about how she would have left her husband if it hadn't been for the children. It would have upset me because I didn't know how to fit her in my Panama story. *When the little bear and the little tiger asked for the way to Panama, all the animals told them to turn left.* I wouldn't have cared if May had told me to turn left or right. I just hated to hear that she was stuck in-between.

I started saying "no" to May when she asked to use my computer. Sometimes, I even ignored her phone calls. One night, she left me a voicemail when I didn't pick up the phone. She sounded terrified and said that she needed to borrow around fifty dollars. I returned her call, but she didn't answer. I left a message saying she could come over. She didn't show up and I didn't see her working in her small yard the following week. I was a bit worried about her.

The next time I saw her wiping the windows, I made sure to greet her.

"Hi," I said. "How was your week?" I tried to sound as casual as possible.

"Boring," she said, "nothing happened." She looked straight at me. She could read my mind.

"Where have you been?" I asked.

"I went to my relative's house," she said. "I just needed some cash to pay for the toll bridge. I don't have a credit card. My husband left me some cash for groceries, but that's all. I wanted to apply for a credit card, but I don't have any credit history. My husband didn't want to vouch for me."

That explained why she was selling cookies. Her husband paid for the ingredients. He never wondered why his household consumed so much flour, sugar, and butter.

Before that visit, I made sure to bring last month's telephone bill with me. There were fees from her long distance calls. One call was made to Queens and two calls were made to Indonesia. Although I needed to ask May for five dollars, I cut her story short. I didn't have the patience for a depressing story. I left her in such a brutal hurry that I never had the chance to ask her for the money that she owed me.

May died the same day I moved out of my Avenel house. I saw police cars parked outside her small yard and an old woman stepping out of May's door carrying May's one-year-old baby in her arms. May's three-year-old toddler followed behind the old woman. The windows were still dust-free, but the curtains were drawn closed. I couldn't see anything through the windows, except my own reflection. I didn't ask anyone what happened and I didn't want to know.

The day before, I hired May to help me clean my house. My house was generally well-kept and it couldn't have been that difficult to restore it to the way it looked when I first moved in, of course, other than the mess made by the disaster. The disaster happened because I tried to roast a duck. I ended up roasting the kitchen instead. I should also add, it started from a craving I had for the special type of roasted duck my mother used to make me. I called my mom one winter afternoon and asked her for the recipe. She generously gave it to me. In the spirit of generosity, she offered to talk me through the process. I hastily hung up because I needed to buy tortillas, so I put the duck in the oven and went grocery shopping. While I was away, something happened to the duck and turned it into a mass of charcoal. Smoke from the oven triggered the fire alarm. My next-door Indian neighbors were so scared that they ran out of their house and huddled together in the street.

My mother heard about the disaster and insisted that I shouldn't have hung up so early. She said that I should have listened to her whole story.

Anyway, my house, especially my kitchen, needed a huge cleaning. It was a task beyond my ability, so I looked for cleaning services. May heard about it and offered to help. I told May that I didn't want help from a friend. Instead, I wanted service from a professional company. May said that she desperately needed cash. "You've got to help me," she said. "It is a matter of life and death. Whoever gives you a quote, I can beat it, and I can do as good of a job as anyone else."

She brushed and scraped in a crazy way, as if she were a machine that had no brain. The next day, when I heard May died, I kept thinking about the last image she left in my mind. Her face, her arms, and her frock were covered in soot. When I put the money in her palm, she grinned broadly and I saw her white teeth flash.

Her hand was warm. I would never pay a friend to do housework. No, I wasn't as sad about her death as you may have imagined. She was not my friend.

Some years later, I went back to China. I returned to the house with the green mailbox that I often dreamed about when I was living in Avenel. There was a grocery store nearby. One evening, I saw the grocery store owner catch a mouse. He put the mouse in a cage and set the entire cage on fire. When I passed the scene, the mouse mystically stopped struggling and gave me a calm look. I lowered my head and tried to walk by as coolly as possible. I tried to quickly divert my attention.

What could I have been thinking about at that moment? I might have been reflecting on the mice in Avenel. They were a tough and stout species. Even if they were caught by a mouse trap or a sticky board, they could still break away after they had been thrown in a garbage bin. No one thought of burning a mouse to death in Avenel.

Actually, I wasn't quite sure that the mouse burning incident happened in my hometown. I can only say for sure that the owner was of Chinese descent. The whole family was Chinese. When it became dark outside, they turned a fruit basket upside down and set dishes on top of it. The only square stool was reserved for the owner's petite yet strong wife. The owner, their school-aged daughter, and their one-year-old son all crouched around the make-shift dining table. They all had chopsticks and bowls in their hands. They always chewed their food with great joy.

Chinese people live all over the world nowadays. The fact that the owner was Chinese doesn't necessarily mean that the store was in my hometown.

The store could be in Avenel. Oh, no. It wasn't likely that it was in that city. Now I clearly remember what happened at the grocery store in Avenel. There was a clerk who had been polite to me the entire year. The day before I moved away, she held my hand and told me to stay. She called her manager and asked me to compliment her one more time in front of him. I remember that the manager had a Texan neck, red and rough. I started speaking warmly with the manager, but somehow the conversation ended with an argument. *You look ugly.* I remember what I said to him. I looked for trouble when I was bored.

Still, I enjoyed my days in Avenel. I had no complaints. I loved the community park. It was not a big park, but Anita's daughter and her friends played soccer there. The broken swing and the tennis court that never got repaired now look so dear in my memory. In the summer evenings, a few old Indian men would sit in lotus positions as though they were in a village meeting. When they spoke to each other, they waved their arms in the air to enhance what they were saying. It seemed as though words were not enough to them, as if they were foreign to each other.

Very far in the distance, beyond the barbed wire, were the woods. Beyond the woods, there was a train track. On the way to the train station, there was a small chicken noodle restaurant. They only served chicken noodle soup. The soup was bland and tasteless. Many people drove a great distance just for that cup of blandness. I saw two police officers inside the restaurant. They lacked the attitude police officers in movies have. They fixed their cold eyes behind the counter and glanced at me without any emotion. They were just like me; they had tasteless chicken noodle soup and then left.

They were probably the two police officers who showed up at May's door.

After I moved back to China, I started dreaming about a house with a balcony. The house wasn't anywhere in particular, the background was hazy, but the house was clear.

Once I saw a bike chained to the balcony. The curtains blocked the inside of the home. The next time I had a dream, the bike was gone and was replaced by a huge Fisher rocking chair. The last time, there was a round patio table with a glass top and a cast iron chair with pretty flowers painted on the back. In the dream, I came by in the morning and saw a woman. She was around my age. She was sitting in the chair and sipping some coffee. I imagined that it would be very tempting to sit on that balcony because one could see what is going on in their neighbor's yard. If it were up to me, I would have chosen a chair made of wood.

The day I left Avenel, Anita's husband drove me to the train station. It was the first and last time that I interacted with him. I had been very busy, of course. I only knew, because Anita told me the first day I met her, that he was twenty years older than his wife.

Anita and her daughter walked me to the Lincoln town car her husband drove. Anita's five-year-old daughter had been getting along with me very well. She wouldn't let go of my hand. She asked me one single question repeatedly, "where are you going?"

I sighed, "To Panama, my dear."

ABOUT THE AUTHOR

JIERU ZHOU was born and raised in Changzhou, Jiangsu Province, China. She came to the United States in 2000 and moved to Hong Kong in 2010. She began her writing career in 1991 and won The Bud Award for Fiction in 1996. She is currently living in Hong Kong and the vice editor-in-chief of *Hong Kong Literature*.

ABOUT THE TRANSLATOR

YING ALEXANDRA CAO is a visual artist based in Los Angeles, California.

Ying Alexandra Cao with Jieru Zhou

Q & A
WITH JIERU ZHOU

After translating "The House in Avenel", Ying Alexandra Cao asked Jieru Zhou nine questions.

Q: I like your story "The House in Avenel". Could you tell me if there is a real house like the one you wrote about?

A: I had been living in America for more than ten years. I moved countless times during my time in the States. I recently finished a novel, *There and Here*, detailing the places I had been through. Avenel is one of the stops where my life paused. It deserved a single chapter. When the editor of *The Strangers* asked me if I had a short story for her to publish, I chose this one. I thought this one was comparatively complete by itself. You don't need that much background information about me to understand it. But, to tell you the truth, all the chapters are equally important to me. Still, Avenel is unique. I assign a different visual comparison to all the places I have lived so that I won't forget them. Avenel is like a moon which is capable of snowing, silent snowing.

Q: It sounds fascinating. What other places did you write about in *There and Here*?

A: For instance, Newport. I moved to Newport right after I moved out from Avenel. In my visual system, Newport is like a huge freezer, which is full of frozen food, fish, fruits, New York cheesecake, you name it.

Q: The experiences in Avenel mainly consist of the narrator's encounter with two women, Anita and May. Is it true that people are the most memorable things for you wherever you live?

A: Yes. My takeaway from life is always about my interaction with people, and my intricate relationships with people always empowers me. Some people were only in my life for a brief amount of time, but their influence persisted. Whenever I think about a place, the people I met there always pop up first. But, I am not going to say that what I wrote in my story is the same as what happened in real life. Those are two different things.

Q: You quote Janosch's *The Trip to Panama* in your story. How did this children's story inspire you?

A: I first heard this story from one of my editors. We worked together on my novel, *The Chinese Doll*. She is a petite girl, and she has a powerful mind. It was at the reception after the book launch that she told me about Janosch's story. I remember it clearly because she cried after she finished it. I didn't. I didn't feel particularly touched by it at that time. That was in 2002. When I wrote "The House in Avenel" in 2015, I somehow recalled this story, and finally, I cried too.

Q: Do you feel that writing in English is difficult?

A: Yes, I do. The only occasions when I can use English with confidence is when I am shopping, especially in Hong Kong, where you would receive a much warmer response when you speak English with an accent than when you speak Cantonese with an accent. But it is hard for me to write in English or deliver a speech in English. I am not good at the rhythm. What makes Chinese people's English sound off? Not only because of the accent, but also because of the rhythm. Quite often, we pause at the wrong places. Native English speakers also pause, but they pause at the places where other native English speakers would pause as well.

Q: Are you going to write in English in the future?

A: Perhaps, but I don't think I'll be able to make a living by writing stories in English in my lifetime. I can do translation though, translating English articles into Chinese. In the summer of 2015, I translated an interview about an artist from English to Chinese. It was a 2000-word piece and it took me three days and three nights. It only takes me one hour to write 2000 Chinese characters if it is creative writing. Of course, the main difficulty was in art history, which is foreign to me. All the English terms about colors and materials drove me crazy.

Q: Do you feel the necessity, the urge to speak to English readers?

A: I think the English book market is much more mature than the Chinese book market. There is not much room for strangers to break into. English book reviews are also much more serious than Chinese ones. If a reviewer doesn't like your book, he/she either neglects you or criticizes you, no matter how close a friend you are to him or her or how much you pay him or her. In China, things are different. Reviewers praise books not worth reading to return favors offered by publishers or authors. Readers generally think of themselves as smart and don't trust book reviews, but they'll be tricked into buying worthless books from time to time. The Chinese book market is now like a one-night-stand, and I really don't like it. It is easy to lose yourself there. That's why I'd like to try the water. I want to see if I can be accepted by a serious, mature book market.

Q: Can you tell me something about your favorite English novelist(s)?

A: I had been living in the Bay Area, California, for four years. I can even speak a little Spanish. I am fascinated by Mexican culture, Day of the Dead costumes, and the lethal and exuberant imagery. But I've never been to Mexico and people are always attracted by things they don't have. My favorite English novelist is Sandra Cisneros. I like her narration on cruel childhood. I like the rhythm of her language. I can feel a strong and mysterious connection with her. It has been fifteen years since I read that book, but sometimes I still randomly utter Esperanza for no reason and then I'd be startled. Esperanza is the name of the protagonist in Cisneros' book, *The House on Mango Street*. Esperanza immigrates from Mexico to Chicago. She has survived various tragedies and difficulties, but she never stops searching for a more meaningful life, and she grows up. I like the sound of Esperanza. When I speak the name, I feel like a flower is blossoming at the tip of my tongue.

Q: Ideally, where would you like to live?

A: I guess I'd like to live on Mars. I can enjoy my loneliness and grow my own potatoes.

(Translated by Anna Wang Yuan)

THE GOLDEN VENTURE

by Yili

The old man received a phone call from his daughter-in-law, Jasmine, who told him that she was on her way to America.

"Are you alright?" his wife asked after he hung up the phone. With her glasses on, she was knitting a sweater underneath the lamp.

His stomach was churning acid. His mouth felt dry. The old man mutely gazed at his wife's graying temples. He thought her temples looked like roofs covered by morning frost.

His wife of fifty years went to the kitchen to bring him some tea. She dragged her slippers noisily on the floor. Her body was short and stout and her back was bent over from dull, familiar pain.

While his wife was in the kitchen, the old man's eyes idly drifted to the desk lamp. The dim light took his memory back to the small village in southern China where he grew up. When he was young, the village didn't even have electricity. At their night banquets, the villagers burned gas lamps, which would attract moths. One after another, moths emerged from the dark and charged towards the light without knowing they would be burned into dark corpses and swept away the next morning.

"I tried to stop her. She wouldn't listen," he mumbled, although he was sure that his wife must have heard every word he spoke to

Jasmine. Their bachelor studio was very small. After putting in a queen-sized bed, a desk and two chairs, they couldn't avoid bumping into each other when they moved around.

A huge crashing sound came from a truck outside on the street. They lived in a basement in the Bronx, New York. Any noise from the street seemed to be amplified. The noise gave him a headache. His wife covered her ears with her hands, as if she could block herself from the world outside.

"It's natural," she sighed, "people at home always think that America is a paradise. Didn't we think the same way?" Her words were almost mesmerizing.

Of course, he never forgot their own excitement when they first learned that they had received their visas so they could immigrate to America. His eldest sister in America applied for their immigrant visas ten years earlier. Just as he became desperate and thought he would never be able to live in America, their applications were granted. When the news spread in the village, their gate almost broke because people were swarming to congratulate them. His small courtyard was packed with extended family members, friends, and neighbors.

"Old pal, you're so lucky! You're heading for paradise." Remarks such as that were repeated countless times that evening.

However, one of his old friends had a different opinion. "You are already seventy years old. It will be hard to start a new life!"

"We are doing this for our sons." He looked indulgingly at his younger son, Little Xuan. *He is twenty-eight years old now, and he has remained single because he wants his dad to get him out of the country.* The old man thought.

"You are doing this for your sons and your grandsons," a young female's voice rose above the crowd. It was Jasmine, the wife of his elder son, Min Xuan. She had been busying herself with serving tea and snacks to the crowd. She put down a dish of sunflower seeds on the table beside him. She did this with a certain amount of force and successfully directed the old man's attention to Min Xuan.

Min Xuan was three years older than Little Xuan. He married Jasmine seven years ago. The young couple's lavish wedding banquet would probably go down in village history. The old man not only paid for the wedding, but also built a three-story house for them with granite countertops in the bathrooms and kitchen. He thought that he treated Jasmine well. Actually, the young couple's life was pretty easy. Min Xuan farmed on their five-acre crop field, and Jasmine ran a grocery store on the ground floor of their house. They had two children, aged three and five.

"Well," he said, "your income has been good. I'll wire money back home . . . . "

"But the dream of going to America has always been in my mind, Papa." Jasmine interrupted him. "Look at the people who have returned from America," she continued. "They all display an air of wealth and importance, don't they? I want my sons to become big shots, too, Papa!"

"Right," he said, "right."

He understood Jasmine. He, too, wanted the best things in the world for his sons and grandsons. It was just that reality was so different from their fantasy.

A year ago, they landed in New York. At first, his relatives, including his three sisters, many cousins, nephews, and nieces, welcomed them with lavish banquets. Once it was over, all the relatives went back to their own busy lives. His eldest sister, who had spent ten years trying to get him to America, was now seventy-five years old. She still had to help out with taking care of her two grandchildren, cleaning, and cooking. The old man's cousin helped the couple find and rent an apartment. He helped furnish their place with some second-hand furniture and then disappeared. The old man spent the rest of his money on a lawyer to help with Little Xuan's immigration application.

During their second week in America, he and his wife started working six days a week at a sewing factory. They were born and reared as farmers, so they were not afraid of hard work. The problem was that they could not predict their future, nor could they predict the future for their sons and grandsons. Years ago, the old man thought willfully that their sacrifice could bring their descendants to the land of hope. But after several encounters with the young gangsters in the Chinese community and having witnessed younger generations drop out of school and carry out miserable lives like their fathers, he began to doubt his vision.

That's the real reason why he had been stalling Jasmine's repeated request to bring his grandsons to America. But, to his astonishment, the pushy, willful Jasmine lost her patience and decided to take matters into her own hands.

"Papa, the snakeheads[1] agreed to smuggle me into the States without payment in advance. Please get thirty-five thousand dollars ready for me when I get to New York. Please, for the sake of your grandsons." When Jasmine announced her plan over the phone, she had already left the village. The old man had no way to stop her. He could not verify her whereabouts.

"Where are we going to borrow thirty-five thousand dollars? It's impossible!" He held the teacup that his wife handed to him. The cup was hot, but he didn't feel any warmth. He was shivering.

"Our grandson is six and our granddaughter is four," the old man's wife said. "Jasmine shouldn't have left them for Min Xuan

---

[1]Chinese gangs that smuggle people into other countries.

to take care of. How will he be able to handle them both, take care of the field, and run the store?" His wife's eyes were full of concern. "Well, I am going back to China. I am not used to living here, anyway. My health is deteriorating. My arthritis is worsening."

"If you go home, I'll go with you. Let's count our change and buy the airplane tickets tomorrow," he said in a slightly sarcastic tone.

His wife was quiet. They had saved three thousand two hundred and sixty-four dollars so far. If they spent the money on plane tickets and gifts for the villagers, it would mean that their life savings would return to zero.

They had no other choice but to endure more hardship for their descendants.

Every week, from Monday to Saturday, they worked in Chinatown at a sewing factory. Inside the building, dust floated freely under the bright florescent lights. Thirty sewing machines worked 24 hours a day. The owner, Mr. Liu, had immigrated from their home village many years ago. He was very reluctant to hire the old couple because of their age and inexperience. He gave them a two-month trial period as a gesture to the old man's cousin, to whom he must have owed some favor from a long time ago. The old man's wife earned twenty-five dollars per day, and he earned thirty. Together they made three hundred and thirty dollars every week. His wife's work consisted of cutting threads and hanging and folding clothes. His job was to iron clothes. Both of them worked ten hours per day. From morning to evening, the old man stood in front of an ironing board, wearing only a T-shirt and a pair of shorts. Sweat ran down his forehead and his back. By the end of the day, his right hand would feel as if it were filled with lead. However, he survived the trial period, even though his belt moved closer by two holes. He simply did a better job than the stronger and younger men. As a symbol of recognition, Mr. Liu began calling him "uncle". All went well, except that he didn't know how long he could continue with this hard work.

One Sunday afternoon, the old couple knocked on the door of a three-story house in Queens, where the old man's eldest sister lived.

It was the first time they had asked for help since they arrived in America. After they had stated their intention to borrow money, his sister flatly rejected the request.

"I'd help you if I had the money myself. You know that I am living off my son's support, don't you? And even my son wouldn't help me for nothing. I am practically a nanny, a maid, and a cook in this house." She shrugged and said bitterly. "Besides, Hui's restaurant is doing poorly. He had to let go of three workers."

Hui was her eldest son. He owned a big restaurant. The old man's sister threw her hands in the air, showing her despair. The old man's eyes followed her gesture involuntarily and saw the majestic crystal chandelier hanging from the ceiling. The shiny, intricate crystal made him dizzy.

"Big sister, you've got to help me. The snakeheads will kill Jasmine if I can't pay." He knew his sister wasn't as broke as she described. She must have some savings of her own.

"I did have some pocket money myself, but Ling borrowed twenty thousand from me last month. My savings are mostly gone." It took the old man several seconds to remember that Ling was his sister's second daughter. "Two of her husband's relatives had arrived last month. They needed to pay the snakeheads, too. Can you imagine paying seventy thousand in cash? Of course, it is her husband's duty to sort out the mess. But when your daughter marries the wrong guy, you have no choice but to act as a safety net."

Hui's wife, Yun, came out of nowhere and said, "When the killers come up to your doorstep, they simply kill the whole household. They don't bother figuring out who owes them money, or so I've heard."

The old man turned to Yun. "Do you think the snakeheads would allow us to pay them in installments?"

"How should I know?" Yun shrugged. "What I've heard is that not everyone can get to the States successfully. You don't have to pay if Jasmine dies on the way to America."

"Stop that!" The old man's sister glared at her daughter-in-law.

"I don't mind, big sister," the old man raised one hand, as if to protect Yun from her mother-in-law. "Please tell me, what could happen to Jasmine?"

"I've heard that the trip is extremely dangerous." Yun spoke in a slightly excited way. "Some have physically collapsed, some were abandoned, some drowned, some had to climb mountains, and some were attacked by tigers."

"Amitofo—" his eldest sister chanted a Buddhist blessing loudly.

"It's true." Yun was in her element, perhaps because she did not have enough listeners on a daily basis. "Lots of people just disappeared. It wouldn't be a surprise to find people dead in the truck. I read in the paper that some women were raped and dumped in the desert. Some were forced to become prostitutes if their families couldn't pay the ransom."

"Yun, go get some cookies, please!" his sister ordered sternly.

The old man's heart was thumping hard. His wife looked livid.

Their next plan was to ask the old man's cousin for money. His cousin had been in the U.S. for over thirty years and was quite successful. He used to run a laundry business. After he sold his shop, he started lending money with high interest rates.

The cousin and the old man had grown up together in the same village. When the old couple first arrived in New York, he had reached out to them with a helping hand, but that was all. The old man knew perfectly well that his cousin was more emotionally removed from him than his big sister. So, when he approached his cousin, he tried to act in a professional manner. He put together a repayment plan and presented it to him up front. *We can pay you back in five years. Jasmine is young and strong. The three of us could make fifteen thousand a year.*

"We are not short of young and strong people. We are short of jobs," his cousin shook his head. He had a worried look written all over his face. "I think it is getting harder to find jobs. The economy has been bad. People are fresh off the boat, uneducated, and can't speak English. It's getting harder and harder to make a living."

He then went on to make an eloquent speech. "These Chinese illegal immigrants are getting out of hand. They don't scout the ground before getting into a battle. They are like moths flying right into the flame. I'd like to help you, but lately everyone has felt the pinch. If I helped pay for one cousin, do you have an idea how many more cousins, nephews, nieces, uncles would be coming my way? Even the thought of it is giving me a headache." He used his index finger to tap his forehead for emphasis.

"Do you have any idea how many people have been smuggled here in the past year?" The old man asked cautiously.

His cousin looked around and whispered, "Two ships a month."

"Ah," the old man uttered a cry and then went silent.

His cousin puffed through his nose. "You are worrying about your own job, aren't you?"

It was true. The old man knew perfectly well that no matter how diligently he worked, the bottom line was that he's no competition for stronger and younger men.

"You know what you did wrong?" his cousin went back to his sumptuous air. "You should have changed your phone number earlier."

"Why?"

"She would not have dared to leave if she didn't have a way to reach you. A lot of people change their numbers when their relatives in China start calling them."

"But it's too late, isn't it?"

"Not at all. If she can't reach you, she will turn around and go back to the village no matter how far she's already gone. Trust me, I can read these young people's minds."

The couple left with the cousin's advice. At first, they thought it was ridiculous to change their phone number, but the idea floated around, and like bacteria, the thoughts began to multiply.

Their second winter in New York seemed endless.

The long ride on the subway took an hour from the Bronx every morning. Normally it would also take them fifteen minutes to walk to the subway station, but the snow doubled their walking time because they had to walk very cautiously on the slushy pavements. His wife had arthritic knees, and she was terrified of falling. She clung tightly to the old man's arm while cursing at the snow with each step. It seemed that the white, innocent snow slowly turned black and ominous under her curse. The snowstorms arrived one after another. The snow and ice kept piling by the roadside.

It was still dark when they left their home in the morning. Their relatives had told them that they should have twenty dollars in their pockets at all times. *If you were robbed by a drug addict, a twenty-dollar bill could save your lives.* However, they only carried their monthly passes for the subway, plus a few dollars, no matter what. *A twenty-dollar bill is more dear to us than our own lives, believe it or not!*

After a day's work and long hours of commuting, they only had eight or nine hours to themselves. In order to save money, they cooked their own meals. The old man's wife knitted all sorts of winter clothing such as sweaters, scarves, and mittens. Luckily, they only needed four to five hours of sleep. However, all the warm clothing could not protect them from the cold weather. His wife continued to have a runny nose and headaches, and he had developed a persistent cough. They had taken a lot of herbal medicine without relief. They decided to seek western medical help. The doctor's fees and the medicine cost them two hundred dollars, which amounted to two weeks' worth of their savings. The doctor asked them to return in a week for follow-up check-ups. His wife proclaimed that she would never step into the clinic again as long as she was still breathing; she would rather drop dead on the street.

At their weakest moments, a thought flashed across the couple's mind. What if they changed their telephone numbers? After all, it was Jasmine who put herself into this precarious situation by being aggressive. The old man thought it over on the subway one day. He wanted to bring it up with his wife, but he was too tired to speak. Another day, his wife thought about saying something to her husband. But once they arrived home, she immediately began washing clothes and cooking. They did not have time for conversation. They were either too busy or too tired. The thought of abandoning Jasmine popped up occasionally and then dissipated like a mound of bubbles.

Jasmine called again. She was already in Thailand, and she sounded cheerful and hopeful.

"Papa, do you have the money ready? I shall arrive in New York in one month."

He did not know how to respond. He wished that he could rob a bank.

At last, it occurred to the old man that he could probably borrow money from his Home Town Association.

The couple's Home Town Association was something between a union and a club. On Sundays, many people came to the Association Hall to play Mahjong. It was a very noisy place. You could hear shouting in foreign dialects, laughter, and the clicking of Mahjong blocks. Most people were retirees who wanted to pass the time. They gambled, but in a mild, leisurely way. Occasionally a couple of novices came to the Association Hall and wanted to win big, but their ambition would soon be dampened by the way the regulars would unite and fight against the new aggressor.

At the end of each month, they had something called a "money gathering." It was run like a credit union. Each member of a group would put in a few hundred dollars per month. He or she who needed cash the most would bid the highest interest that month. Once the person received the money, they would pay the principle and the interest back in installments in the following months. Some people who had extra cash on hand preferred to put their money here instead of depositing it in a bank account. That way, they could avoid paying income tax on earned interest.

The old man decided to join the fifty-people group and get cash to pay for Jasmine's trip. This meant that he would be in debt for the next five years. Hopefully once Jasmine arrived, she would find a job and pay it off herself. He did not think that he could work five more years.

Jasmine's next call was made just as the snow began to thaw. She sounded terrified, "Papa, we haven't been able to find a boat.

The snakeheads changed their mind and asked us to pay up front. They are threatening to sell me to the local brothel if I can't pay them now."

"I've already got the money ready," the old man said.

"Have you? Have you?" Jasmine twittered in excitement, "you're so great, Papa! I love you!"

It was the most memorable conversation he'd ever had with anyone from the younger generation. Neither Little Xuan nor Min Xuan had ever expressed their gratefulness to him so effusively. He felt warmth springing up from the bottom of his heart. *It is worth it.* He thought. "You take care of yourself," the old man said before he hung up.

When the old couple went back home the next evening, they found a young man waiting for them at the entrance of their basement. He wore a thick jacket, but pulled his sleeve up to exhibit a dragon tattoo on his left forearm despite the chilly weather in April. He claimed that he was sent to collect the payment. When the old couple entered their crammed bachelor studio, he followed closely behind and made the space seem even smaller. He watched the old man while the old man took out a stack of money stashed between the mattress and the bed board. He grabbed the money from the old man's shaking hands without any nonsense.

They didn't hear from Jasmine for a long time. The old man knew she had entered the last phase of her trip, which was usually the most dangerous part of the whole journey. He counted the days. When the peach trees began blossoming in May, he started to worry. There was a shoot-out one day in New York's Chinatown. Rumor had it that the snakeheads had a fallout with another gang. As a result, no one was going to receive the shipload of smuggled people.

"Papa, please save me," Jasmine cried, as she was floating in the water, with her head bobbing in the waves and her arms stretched out like two sticks. In his nightmare, the old man was standing at the shore, watching her move farther and farther away. She was finally engulfed by the dark gray waves.

The old man did not dare talk about his worries with his wife because he knew she was even more anxious than he was. She made a few secret visits to the Buddhist temple in Chinatown to pray for Jasmine's safety. She also squandered twenty dollars on a fortune-teller to inquire about Jasmine's destiny. The fortune-teller's words were vague.

One day in mid 1993, the phone rang just as they returned from work. The old man ran to grab the phone. It was his eldest sister.

"Did you know that more than two-hundred Chinese illegal immigrants got caught on a ship off the New York Harbor?

"When did this happen? Do they have a list of names?"

"I don't know. It was on TV. Yun told me about it. Do you think Jasmine was on the boat?"

He could feel sweat dripping down his forehead. "Big sister, she left China five months ago. If she was among this group, it'd be a blessing. At least it would mean that she's still alive. Please help me find out how the immigration office will handle this case. I am useless."

"I am as useless as you are," his sister sighed. "Why don't you read the newspaper yourself?"

From that day on, he and his wife walked an extra mile to a grocery store every evening on their way home. The grocery store discounted the daily Chinese newspaper after 6 p.m.

He found out from the Chinese newspaper that the ship was named The Golden Venture. What an ironic name! The Golden

Venture had had all the bad luck in the world. When it stalled near the shore, some of the young men jumped off the ship in desperation. A few people drowned. The coastal guards spotted the ship and took all the passengers, more than two hundred and eighty people, to jail. Unfortunately, the newspapers did not provide a full list of the passengers on board.

The old couple formed a habit of wandering in electronics stores during the evenings. They looked for TVs switched to a news channel and stared at the screen for a long time. They saw the passengers at the beach, sitting in rows with their heads bent down and shivering in the cold. They saw them being escorted to a bus, and the bus entered a gate topped with barbed wire. Finally, they saw the backs of some women. The old man and his wife wondered if one of them could be Jasmine.

Every Sunday, they went to the Home Town Association. It turned out to be their best news source. They found out that some American lawyers were assisting the detainees by helping them apply for political asylum. That was a surprise to the old couple. They thought Americans would not welcome them because these days, they often encountered people who shouted, "Go back to China!" while throwing firecrackers at them.

Six months passed. One winter night, when they went home, they found a young man with fair hair and blue eyes waiting for them at the entrance of their basement.

"What do you want from us?" The old man could speak one or two sentences of English now.

The young man smiled and said something in English beyond the old couple's comprehension. The old man and his wife looked at each other and shook their heads. The young man handed an envelope to them and waited at the door.

It was a letter written by Jasmine. "Papa, I'm in jail." The old man read the first sentence. He and his wife hugged each other and cried out joyfully.

In the letter, Jasmine told them that she was in jail, but she could not describe the location. The American government gave them two options: be deported back to China or stay in jail for God knows how long. She was allowed to call them once, but no one had answered the phone. In the end, she decided to stay in jail because it wasn't too bad. She and some other women made a Mahjong set with papier-mâché last week. All sorts of religious people came to visit them. She took every chance to talk with the visitors, whether it be a Christian priest or a Buddhist monk. At the end of the letter, Jasmine asked for five hundred dollars because she needed to buy some toiletries and warm clothes.

The old couple did not know if they should cry or laugh when they finished reading Jasmine's letter. It seemed that she was living a more comfortable life than they were. Grudgingly, the old man pulled out some twenty-dollar bills, sealed them in an envelope, and gave it to the young man.

Relieved that Jasmine was safe, the old couple carried on with their daily routine. They could not do anything except wait patiently. At first, they'd talk about Jasmine's fate every day, but then they became tired of repeating the same conversation. They grew more and more silent. On Sundays they stayed home all day just in case Jasmine called them again. Every time the phone rang, they'd run to it. They were disappointed every time because it was never Jasmine.

Another six months had gone by, but nothing happened. One more year went by, and still nothing happened. Somewhere in the third year of Jasmine's incarceration, Min Xuan called them. He told the couple that Jasmine had written to let him know that she was going to divorce him. The old man was puzzled at first. But, if he had learned one thing from recent years, it was that he couldn't understand the younger generation any more. Later he learned from someone that some detainees applied for political asylum. Was Jasmine one of them?

One day in February 1997, four years after The Golden Venture incident, the old man's eldest sister called him. "Have you heard that the rest of the detainees are going to be released today?"

"Really?" the old man could not believe his ears. "Can we go to your house and watch the news?"

"Sure," his sister agreed.

The old man and his wife traveled halfway through the city and knocked on his sister's door around midnight. His sister turned on the TV and muted it. None of them could understand any words that the news anchor said, anyway. The old couple stared at the screen without blinking for a few seconds. They saw a dozen young Chinese men, all in white pants and blue sweaters, walk out of a prison. The camera turned and they saw a group of American volunteers clapping and welcoming the newly released people.

There weren't any females; they did not see Jasmine.

"I've heard they were detained in different jails," his sister consoled him. "You'd better go home now. Jasmine could be knocking on your door any minute."

They went back home with hope. They wondered how they were going to face Jasmine. Had she divorced her husband, Min Xuan? They heard nothing from her after Min Xuan's last call. Most likely she did not apply for political asylum, because that would have cost a lot of legal fees. Should they ask her to pay back the thirty-five thousand dollars?

"She's young and can find work," the old man said to his wife. "She's gone through so much. I think we should allow her to make a new life for herself."

"But we need the money," his wife protested. "Little Xuan's immigration application could be granted any day. He is going to need money to start his family."

The next morning, when the couple were ready to go to work, they opened the door. There at the doorstep, was Jasmine sitting with her small suitcase. She looked exactly the same as they remembered. No, she looked even stronger and healthier. What remained unchanged were her eyes. They were wide and full of curiosity.

"Papa! Mama!" Jasmine cried.

"Jasmine, how did you get here?" the old man cried.

"A volunteer drove me here," Jasmine said cheerfully. "Thank God I don't have to go back to China!"

"Come on in, Jasmine." The old man's wife led the way.

Jasmine followed the old couple and looked around in an inquisitive manner. "Papa, Mama, why do you live in the basement? It is so stuffy in here...Papa, did you lose weight? Are you sick? Look at me. Even I've put on a few pounds, and I've been in jail."

The old man wanted to say something, but before he uttered any words, Jasmine shot out more questions again. "Is it true that I could make at least one or two thousand dollars a month? I can't wait to start working. Please help me find a job."

The old man and his wife looked at each other and decided to remain silent. Jasmine had finally arrived. That was all. They did not need to say anything more. She would find out for herself what America was like. She could decide whether America was bitter or sweet.

YILI was born in Wenzhou, Zhejiang Province, China. She immigrated to Hong Kong at the age of ten and moved to Paris after graduating from high school. She went to England the following year and moved to Boston in 1973. She studied English literature at the University of Massachusetts and creative writing at San Francisco State University. For many years, she worked in a Chinese community center and helped immigrants settle in a new country. Her writing career started with stories about these immigrants. She writes about their struggle for survival and the lasting clash between Eastern and Western cultures. She has published collections of short stories, novels, and collections of essays in Hong Kong, Taiwan, and China. She is a lifetime member of the Overseas Chinese Women Writers' Association and an advisory board member of The Way Literary Association. She currently writes blogs for websites such as the *World Journal* and *Creaders*.

Yili loves nature and enjoys traveling.

Q & A
WITH YILI

Jin Hui, the reporter of *Wenzhou City News*, asked Yili five questions when Yili visited her hometown, Wenzhou, Zhejiang Province, China, in 2011. The interview was first published in Chinese in *Wenzhou City News* on November 10th, 2011.

Q: You are a writer from Wenzhou. Can you tell me about some memories of your hometown?

A: Wenzhou is my hometown, but I left when I was ten. My memory about my hometown is fuzzy. I remember that the mountain village where I was born was very small and it was surrounded by a forest of bamboo. There was hardly any means of transportation. In fact, there was next to zero. The villagers' lives were totally at the mercy of nature. Thirty years later, I returned to my hometown with my children. We were shocked by the scene in front of us. It was incredible to think of the long way I had gone. My daughter asked me to describe the toys that I had played with during my childhood, and I couldn't think of any.

Q: Having been born in Wenzhou and having Wenzhou heritage, do you feel that you are different when you are living overseas?

A: After leaving Wenzhou, I first went to Hong Kong. It was in the late 1950s and there were very few people from Wenzhou in Hong Kong. I left Hong Kong for France after I graduated from high school and surprisingly, I found an active Wenzhou community in Paris. Wenzhou people are known for their hard work and business instincts. The Wenzhou people in Paris carry their "Wenzhouness" forward to the fullest extent. Moreover, they take care of each other. My identity of being a Wenzhou descendent was established when I was in Paris. I am very proud that I have Wenzhou heritage to this day.

Q: You went to college after you got married. I understand it was not a very easy decision for you and your family. Can you tell me something about your husband? Are there any romantic stories between you two?

A: My husband is also from Wenzhou. He left Wenzhou for Hong Kong when he was seven, just like me, but we didn't meet each other when we were both in Hong Kong. After high school, he went to the University of California at Berkeley to study physics. Our path had never really crossed except for the fact that we were both born in Wenzhou. Both of our parents hoped their children could find a spouse from their hometown, so they arranged for us to write to each other. When I first received his letter from the States, I didn't think of him as my future husband. I just took him as a pen pal. Once, I sent him a piece of my published article, and he expressed his appreciation toward it. He also told me that he loved literature and he was a voracious reader, too. Our mutual understanding hence deepened. After we got married, he supported me so I could study English Literature at the University of Massachusetts. He was doing post-doc research at that time and he didn't earn much money. Neither of us desired many material things in our lives. We couldn't afford a car. But we were happy as long as we could pursue our dreams.

Q: You majored in English literature, but you started off writing in Chinese instead of writing in English. Why is that?

A: I studied English literature for three years, but it was different writing in English than reading in English. I tried writing in English for a while, but I didn't have any hope that my stories written in English would be published. Meanwhile, I submitted my stories written in Chinese to newspapers and magazines based in Hong Kong and they were accepted. I was encouraged and went on to submit my stories to Chinese newspapers based in the States. They were accepted, too. In the 1970s, there were not many overseas Chinese writers and my writings were met with warm responses. Over the years, my writings were published in various places, including Taiwan and mainland China.

Q: Your writing career has been mentioned in books and research papers, such as *The History of Overseas Chinese Literature* and *A Course in Taiwan, Hong Kong, Macau and Overseas Chinese Literature.* Could you please tell me what you think of your own writings?

A: That is a hard question. I don't know how to judge my own work objectively. I am a writer. Whenever I hear a story, if it is good, if it touches me, I'll tell myself to write it down. My subject matter is mainly about immigrants, like the predicaments that new immigrants must face, or the lasting struggle between the new and the old worlds. One signature throughout my stories is that I mainly write about working class immigrants. Therefore, in a sense, I differentiate myself from the majority of overseas Chinese writers who write about students and scholars.

(Translated by Anna Wang Yuan)

THE
STRANGERS

PART 3

"I opened myself to the gentle indifference of the world."

— Albert Camus
The Stranger

VACANCES À PARIS

by Christina Yao

Only one of us could attend the annual cancer genetics meeting in Paris due to limited traveling funds in our research lab. My boss, Franklin Richard, picked me because he thought I needed a vacation. My colleague, Nancy, was happy that I could leave my family and work behind for a short break.

"Ping, you don't have a life." She had been saying the same stuff over and over again to me for four years. "Do all Chinese people work so hard?" she smiled, with a hint of teasing.

I answered in a matter-of-fact way, "Yes." I knew I wasn't a person who was fun to be around, but who cares?

I took a cab from the airport to my hotel. I looked out the taxi window and saw beautiful Parisian greenery everywhere. I realized that green was something I was missing in New York City. *Is that why New Yorkers look so pale?* I thought. I got more pale every day. Now, I began to understand Nancy's comment, "Ping, you don't have a life." She meant that my life was so crowded with things-to-do that I did not have a moment to myself.

Everything is fine with me, especially my career. I finished my Ph.D. at Johns Hopkins University and spent two years working on my postdoc at Yale. Afterwards, I moved to New York to work at a medical center. Realizing that the only way to get respect was to excel in my work, I hadn't seen a movie or read a novel in four years. I have a family—a husband and a daughter. If I am not in the office or laboratory, I am commuting in a smelly subway or doing housework at home. I have no time or energy to desire anything else. Still, when Nancy asked me whether I had a life, she made me upset.

"Where are you from?" the pleasant, chubby driver suddenly asked me.

"China." Even after I received my U.S. citizenship, I still had trouble claiming that I was as an American. I was afraid I would be asked, "Why don't you go back to China?"

Xue-Fei, my husband, wanted to return to China. He was getting more and more upset that our daughter, Xiao-Jie, spoke perfect English, but very little Chinese. I think the real reason why he felt unsettled was that he couldn't find his place in the States.

"China? My wife, Chinese, too." The driver stared at me for a few seconds then commented, "Chinese women, beautiful. Good cooks, too."

I hate being stereotyped. Yet, I understood that he said it as a compliment. I remained silent.

Xue-Fei and I met at Beijing Medical University. I was eighteen and he was nineteen. The first time we met, I was attracted to him. His dark eyes stole my heart. I waited for a signal from him, but it never came. Xue-Fei was too shy to express his emotions, probably because I was one of the best students in the class. One day, I organized a group trip to the Xiang-Shan Park to see the maple trees. Xue-Fei and some of his friends refused to go. I went to his dormitory and asked, "Xue-Fei, why don't you want to go? Wouldn't you like to do something with your classmates?"

"I would rather play volleyball with my friends," Xue-Fei answered, innocently. "Plus, I hardly speak with any girls in our class."

"Okay. If I invite you as a friend, would you go?" I asked.

"A friend?" Xue-Fei looked into my eyes for the first time and then asked, "Are you being sincere?"

"Yes," I said.

Xue-Fei smiled slyly.

We went to the park and saw the autumn maple trees. Xue-Fei asked me whether I thought the leaves looked like blood, fire, or sunsets. I did not like any of his similes. I'd rather be silently thrown into its fiery brilliance. After a long discussion, we finally agreed that the autumn leaves could be a symbol for love.

When it was time to go home, Xue-Fei put me on the back of his bicycle. No words could describe my happiness. It had been my dream to be close to him. As Xue-Fei made a sharp turn, I put my hands around his waist.

"That's the way it should be," he said.

I felt encouraged and asked him if he would like to watch a movie with me. We went to a film called *Tess*. It was an adaptation of a novel written by a British writer, Thomas Hardy. I read some of his poems and truly liked them. It was the 1980s. Chinese people didn't watch a lot of movies with lovers kissing on the screen. It was definitely the first time I saw a man seduce a woman in a film. During the sex scene, Xue-Fei started breathing heavily and my heart began beating fast. That night, in my diary, I declared that I was in love with a man.

What had happened to Xue-Fei? Could this overweight, middle-aged man who drank beers and watched TV most of the time be the same boy I fell in love with fifteen years ago?

Xue-Fei was annoyed by the fact that our daughter, Xiao-Jie, did well in school, but refused to learn our Chinese culture. We often argued about this with each other. Xiao-Jie was born in America, on the Fourth of July. We had no right to force her to live in a traditional Chinese manner. At the end of our fights, Xue-Fei often concluded that we should one day send Xiao-Jie back to China.

"Madame, here is your hotel," the driver informed me. He said goodbye and warned, "Be careful, young lady, Frenchmen are all bad. Don't give them a chance."

What did he mean by "bad?" Was Xue-Fei a bad man? He came to the U.S. for my sake, but he refused to adapt. He had no friends and wished that I wouldn't have any American friends as well. Did he know how disappointed I felt about our marriage? For a long time, I had no desire for sex. Xue-Fei usually ended his orgasm in a minute or two. He then asked, "Are you done? I will get you a clean towel."

I replied to him every time that I was *done,* like it was a job. I knew we were not doing it right ever since we were married, but I couldn't say for sure what was missing between us. Physically speaking, we did all the right things, but I anticipated more in terms of mood, mutual feelings, urge, and…in short, added enjoyment. And deep down in my heart, I knew that my longing for the added enjoyment was my true desire. But I didn't dare start this discussion with Xue-Fei. He seemed to think that a wife's duty was to accept whatever her husband handed down to her. When Nancy spoke about her sexual life during lunch, I was painfully jealous. Sometimes I wondered what life would have been like if I had married some other guy. Then I warned myself: *Who would put up with you, a frigid middle-aged woman who knows nothing apart from your work?*

I went straight to my hotel room. During my shower, I continued thinking about my life. I had always thought Xue-Fei was intelligent and able to achieve anything he wanted. But it turned out that he was not an achiever. He dropped out of the Ph.D. program. "Ping, I don't like writing papers. My brain hurts when I sit in a seminar. The professors bore me. Aren't these good enough reasons?" While he failed academically, Xue-Fei learned to cook and agreed to do the dishes. I knew that for him, it was a big compromise and sacrifice. He did his fair share in the marriage. I couldn't complain. He pretended to be content with his easy life —playing football, being a lab technician, and taking care of the house. Deep down, he knew that he wasn't the man I used to love and look up to. Maybe that's why he didn't give me sexual satisfaction. He wasn't in the mood to please me. Or even worse, he meant to punish me, in the bedroom.

I murmured to myself, "Xue-Fei, I know we have stopped loving each other a long time ago. Why should we stay together?" Then I stirred, as if I had been struck by lightening. I looked around and saw the bright city lights through the windows. I realized that I was in Paris. It must have been the effect of Paris that made my mind derail. I had never thought of leaving Xue-Fei. Even our daughter, Xiao-Jie, wondered why we still stayed together. Last Valentine's Day, Xiao-Jie drew two pink hearts on a card and asked me to give it to Xue-Fei. I said "sure" without thinking. Xiao-Jie then went on to ask me what I saw in her dad. I answered that he cooked delicious food. Twelve-year-old Xiao-Jie looked relieved and left me alone. I turned around and tears rolled down my cheeks.

The next morning, I woke up late. I jumped out of bed and ran to the metro station half a block away. I followed the map and I had no trouble transferring trains. The trouble arrived when I realized that I misplaced my metro ticket. I was searching for it when I heard someone speak to me in French. I looked up and saw a guy with dark brown skin who looked younger than I was. I told him in English that I could not speak French, and I didn't have a ticket.

He gave me his and showed me how to insert it into the slot. I used his ticket but worried about how he would get out. To my surprise, he simply jumped over the turnstile. He also showed me the way to the conference center. At the reception desk, he even got me an updated program. It turned out that he was attending the same conference.

After we found out that the first lecture had been postponed, we sat on a bench in a garden and began chatting. I briefly explained my work in psychiatric genetics. He introduced himself as a second-year medical student. He was going to do clinical research for a year or two and become a surgeon afterwards. Half an hour passed by without either one of us noticing. He then said, "Have we been formally introduced?" I started to laugh. He told me that his name was Tahar. *How interesting!* I thought. *His name sounds like the word "he" in Chinese.* He was amused by my name. "Ping? Do you hit your head against the wall, ping-ping?" I couldn't help but utter a hearty laugh.

It was time for me to deliver a speech about the recent research development on genetic defection. I said goodbye to Tahar and hurried inside the conference center. When I finished my speech and left the conference room, I saw that Tahar was still standing there. He held a program up in the air and waved to me. "Dr. Ping Wu!" He called out and imitated the tone of a fanatic fan. "Please sign my T-shirt!"

The time of lecture-giving had suddenly disappeared. My doctor persona was gone instantly. I totally forgot that several minutes ago, I had been presenting my research results to a roomful of highly-achieved scientists. I returned to the carefree, easy-going girl I had been when I first met Tahar.

"Tahar," I asked, "did you listen to any of the speeches or have you been standing here the whole time?"

He winked at me and answered that he had found the most important thing in his life. To this, I made no reply. He proceeded to invite me to lunch and I agreed.

While we ate, he asked me if I had any other plans while I was in Paris. I told him flatly that my only purpose here was to attend the conference. He made a grimace and it made me laugh again. Somehow I could not keep my demure manner in front of this young man. Laughing was the easiest thing to do when I was with him. So, against all my will, I uttered, "I'd like to visit the Louvre."

"Of course," he said smoothly, as if visiting the Louvre was the most natural thing in the world. "We can do that this weekend."

"We?" I repeated his word involuntarily.

He ignored my question and asked me, "How about dinner?"

"What do you mean by that?" I was truly perplexed. His thoughts were like dots jumping around and I couldn't connect them.

"I mean…" he first looked into my eyes and then looked down at the table. When he looked up at me again, he suddenly changed from a vibrant and confident man to a wishful and vulnerable child. "I want to have dinner with you," he said. His expression reminded me of Xiao-Jie. When my daughter wanted me to put her to sleep, she would ask me with that same kind of expression. I hated to say no to her. I hated to refuse Tahar, too.

"Maybe," I murmured.

"I will not leave you alone unless you promise me." He winked again and said, "Guess what will happen next? Our lunch will be extended to dinner."

"Fine." I surrendered, willingly.

"I'll wait for you at the front door," he said.

"You're acting so much like my daughter." I shook my head.

"Your daughter? Are you a married woman?" His eyes were

wide open. "That's incredible! You look so young!"

"But I'm an old woman, really." I blushed. "Would you like to reconsider your invitation?"

"No," he said. "There isn't a law that forbids me from taking a lovely woman to dinner, married or unmarried, young or old. I don't care."

That night, he took me to a French restaurant in the Latin Square. We sat outdoors at his favorite table. It was a nice evening. I was already drunk before I tasted the cocktail that Tahar ordered for me. Tahar, too, looked tipsy when he raised his glass.

"Was it good?" he asked me after I sipped my liquor.

"Wonderful!" I said.

He was in his element. A young blonde passed by and greeted Tahar in French. He returned her greeting.

"Do you know her?" I asked.

"I know most of the regulars at this restaurant," he said casually.

I looked again at the blonde sitting across several tables. She winked at me and smiled. I had a strange feeling that they had an intimate relationship at some point in their past. I felt a bit jealous. *Who do you think you are?* I sternly warned myself.

"What's the matter?" he asked. He noticed something was wrong.

"Tahar," I looked straight into his eyes. "Tell me the truth, do you always get what you want?"

"Of course not," he said.

"What haven't you received in your past?" I asked.

"A lot of things," he contemplated. "Now, tell me the truth. Are you interested in me or do you only want to have a good time with me?"

I made the only possible answer, "You interest me."

"Well, you're lucky tonight," he said. "I happen to be in the mood to tell you my story."

Tahar told me that he was born in Paris, but his parents were from Nigeria. He told me how he had been trapped in a poor, tough neighborhood during his entire youth. The first time he visited Paris, he thought he must have traveled to a different country. He couldn't identify himself as a Frenchman, even though he was born in France and could speak the language. He was not a French citizen. He concluded, "I do not feel at home here." Then he asked, "How's it like in America?"

I began telling him about my own frustrations very naturally. "I am a naturalized citizen of the United States, but I have difficulty calling myself an American."

He nodded gravely as if every word I said was important to him. I felt encouraged, and as a result, I couldn't stop speaking. Before I realized it, I had told him everything about myself I thought worth mentioning—my work, my daughter, and even Nancy.

When Tahar took me back to the hotel it was almost one o'clock in the morning. He kissed me on my left cheek to say good-bye. "Thank you for a wonderful evening, Ping. I am glad that I met you."

I smiled and turned my back to him. He suddenly grabbed me from behind and turned me around. He kissed me once again, this time on my right cheek.

"Now, you can go," he said. "Sweet dreams."

I could not fall asleep. His kisses lingered on my cheeks. A phrase Nancy often said jumped into my mind—French kiss. *Were those French kisses?* I thought. How I wish Nancy were around! I would ask her about it no matter how hard she would laugh at me. I was sure that she would laugh at my ignorance. But I didn't care because my agitation and anticipation began to overwhelm me. Every cell of my being came to life. I wanted to shout to Nancy, no, to the world, that I had a life! Right here and right now.

But, when I thought about New York, my burning desire was dampened. It seemed that Tahar could only fit in my Paris life. I couldn't picture him being a part of my entire life. I could not place him in the whole picture of my world. How could I introduce him to Xue-Fei or Xiao-Jie? I didn't worry about Nancy, though. I was sure that she could understand everything that was absurd.

How I had survived the next two days was still a mystery to me until now. After the third day's session was over, I saw Tahar waiting for me outside the conference room once again. This time, he took me on a dinner cruise. Unfortunately, it was raining that night, which was not much of a problem to us because we didn't have a spare moment to see the night view anyway. Our eyes were all over each other most of the evening.

Finally, Tahar broke the silence by saying that he fell in love with me.

I was not surprised by his declaration. But, perhaps purely out of the habit of being a scientist, I asked, "How do you define love?"

"I'd like to hold you in my arms. I'd like to kiss you all over your body. I'd like to make love to you all night. I call this kind of desire, love." His eyes sparkled.

I was stunned by his bold and blunt expression. I wasn't used to such a quick revelation.

Tahar, however, grabbed me with his strong arms in spite of my hesitation.

"Oh, no," I murmured in weak protest, "no, no."

"No?" He stopped kissing me.

I didn't want him to stop, but I didn't know how to make a

move myself. I felt like my body and brain were frozen, although I was wrapped in his warm embrace.

He smiled and gingerly kissed me on the lips.

"Was that a French kiss?" I asked. My voice was shaky.

He broke into laughter. He laughed as if I had just told him the funniest joke in the world. After he calmed down, Tahar said, in the most serious tone I'd ever heard from him, "Dr. Ping, would you allow me the opportunity to present you with an authentic French kiss?"

"You are so bad!" I exclaimed. I drummed his chest with my fists.

That night, in my hotel room, I was presented with kisses galore by Tahar. He started with a French kiss, proceeded with what he jokingly called a Nigerian kiss, and then made up what he called a moon kiss. The French kiss was soft, warm, and sentimental. The Nigerian kiss was powerful, passionate, and animal-like. How should I describe the moon kiss? It was simply beyond my words.

"Would you give me a chance to make you happy?" he whispered in my ear.

"What are you talking about?" I was almost out of breath. "You are making me happy."

"That's just the prelude." His naughty signature smile flashed across his face. "I am going to make you happier than before."

"I can't imagine how I can be happier," I sighed. "I have a lack of imagination."

The moment he entered my body, I had the feeling that I was the happiest woman in the world. Nothing can be compared to this moment. Nothing else seemed relevant at this moment. My body was condensed to an imaginary ball of energy. My history was cut short to a time period of no longer than an hour. I was born the moment he entered me. I was burning while he was inside me. I was dead after he retreated from me.

"Hey," he caressed me with his hand, waking me up from my dream little by little.

I opened up my eyes and saw his young, handsome face. Yes, we had fun, but it was over.

I began sobbing.

"What's wrong?" He kissed me again.

"What am I going to do?" I was deeply sad. "Now that I've known there is pleasure in this world."

"We can live together and live happily ever after," he said.

"No, I can't." I said. "I can't leave my husband. He doesn't do anything wrong."

"He doesn't give you the decent sexual life that you deserve," he said. "In my opinion, he is almost a criminal."

I was offended and broke loose from his embrace. "Who told you that?"

"I may not be a successful scientist like you are," he said demurely, "but I am knowledgeable about my favorite subject."

"Still," I said, "I don't think I am eligible for this kind of pleasure."

He asked me to define what I meant by "this kind of pleasure". I thought about it for a while and then said, "I can't put myself above all other responsibilities."

"That's why I desire you," he sighed, a bit desperate. "You are bound. I, on the other hand, am not bound. I am free to fly."

"I envy you." I said.

"Have you ever read *The Unbearable Lightness of Being*?" he said.

"Not yet," I shook my head. "Is it about physics, like *The Brief History of Time*?"

"No," he said. "It's about the choices of life."

In the next few days, I felt as if I were in a dream. We skipped the conference closing sessions and went to the Louvre. When we sat down by the Rodin sculptures, Tahar again begged me to move to Paris. I didn't have the heart to refuse him, but I knew I couldn't make a promise that I wasn't able to keep.

"Is it because of your daughter?" he asked.

"Yes," I said. "No," I overthrew my first answer. I didn't know what I was talking about.

"Please don't break my heart," he said. He put his hand over his chest as if he were protecting his heart.

"Taha…" I said his name out loud for the first time. That name sounded so special to me. *Would I ever be able to forget this name?*

That day, overlooking Paris from the Louvre, Tahar proposed a deal—he was going to borrow a car and drive me to the airport on Monday. I was going to give him my final answer before I boarded the plane. I agreed. Tahar gave me a prolonged French kiss.

I checked out of my hotel Sunday morning. I had changed my plane tickets the day before. I stepped out of the hotel lobby and hailed a taxi. A cab pulled over. The driver rolled down the window and greeted me.

"Hi," he said cheerfully. "Good morning, lovely Chinese lady."

I was surprised. When I looked at him, I realized that he was the same chubby driver who picked me up at the airport a week ago.

"Hello," I greeted him as I climbed into the car.

"Did you find a bad Frenchman?" He drove away from the curb.

"No," I said grimly.

"No, no, no," he shook his head. "You are lying."

"Why?" My heart began to beat fast. Could he have guessed what had happened to me from my appearance?

"You have totally changed into a different person." He paused. "You're younger, more energetic, and more beautiful."

"Thank you," I said. I clammed my mouth throughout the rest of the taxi ride.

I felt a bit dizzy when the airplane took off. For a moment, I was confused by what was going on with me. Is the New York life my destiny—to which I have to return, however disrupted it is? Or is the Paris life my destiny—to which I shall be back, no matter how much time will pass?

Maybe I can investigate more with Nancy. I looked at my reflection in the window and cracked a smile.

CHRISTINA YAO was born and raised in Shanghai, China. She came to the United States to pursue further education in science. She graduated from Columbia University with a doctoral degree in Genetics and now works as an investigator at the National Institutes of Health (NIH). Her specialty is to analyze big data related to the brain, including schizophrenia, bipolar disorder, and obsessive compulsive disorder. While she was studying at Columbia, she enrolled in a writer's program and focused on poetry and short fiction writing. Her literary work has appeared in *Columbia Journal* and *The Baltimore Review*. Her short story "Defection" was included in an anthology, *On a Bed of Rice: An Asian American Erotic Feast* (Ed. Geraldine Kudaka. New York: Anchor Books, 1995). She began creative writing in Chinese a few years ago. Her short stories appeared in a few literature journals in China, including *Shanghai Literature* and *The Literary World* based in Shanghai.

Christina Yao loves nature and enjoys traveling.

Q & A
WITH CHRISTINA YAO

Anna Wang Yuan asked Christina Yao eight questions after editing her short story, "Vacances à Paris".

Q: Your story, "Vacances à Paris", is a rewrite based on your previous published story, "Defection". Could you please describe the history of "Defection"—its creation and its publication?

A: It was very simple. I selected a course on creative writing while I was studying biology at Columbia University. For each term, the students from the writing class were asked to submit three or four short stories. "Defection" was one of my class assignments. My instructor, Raymond Kennedy, thought very highly of this story. He encouraged me to submit it to literary magazines. At first, I didn't take it very seriously. Several months had passed and one day I came upon a "Call for Submissions" from a magazine published by Columbia University. It solicited short stories written by Asian immigrants exploring themes such as sexual awakening, marriage, and interracial love. I thought that my story, "Defection", could fill the bill so I sent it to the editor. After approximately one month, I received a notice telling me that my "Defection" was selected. One of my friends, a Vietnamese girl, congratulated me and commented, "How did you hit the target on your first try? You're such a lucky girl!" The anthology titled *On a Bed of Rice* came out in 1995. As one of the contributors, I was invited to three readings, respectively in New York, San Francisco, and Toronto.

Q: What inspired you to write the story "Defection"?

A: The archetype of the protagonist is one of my friends who is eight years older than me. Her life sparked my curiosity and desire to explore the conundrum faced by many females who immigrated to the U.S. from a comparatively more male-centered country. I met many women just like that in New York. They are smart and hard-working. In a male-dominated society, they would submit themselves to their family, taking care of the house and providing for the needs for their husbands and children. Once they immigrate to a new country where women may have more choices, their lives begin to blossom. But conundrums ensue: how could they balance their newly acquired career and their family life? How could they put up with their husbands if they can't adapt to the new world, or wouldn't keep going at the same speed as their wives in terms of learning the new culture? How could they help their children navigate through cultural conflicts? Although I drew a lot of inspiration from my friend's life, I made sure not to reveal any of her privacy. I could confidently say that the published story was nothing but a work of fiction.

Q: What did you add to "Vacances à Paris"?

A: I added some detailed descriptions about Paris. For instance, I added more words in the restaurant scene, the cruise scene, the hotel scene, etc. I wanted to bump up the alienation felt by Tahar, a second generation Nigerian immigrant, who could speak fluent French, but refused to identify himself as French. That feeling of alienation is shared by Tahar and Ping and is, in my view, the fundamental attraction between the two of them. I was doing revisions when I was hit by the news that a series of coordinated attacks occurred in Paris. I love Paris. It's the most beautiful city in the world. I was shocked and felt sorrow and I suddenly became effusive.

Q: Have you written any other stories apart from "Defection"?

A: Yes. I have five finished stories in my hands. I plan to re-write them this year. Like "Defection", those stories were written nearly twenty years ago. They were mostly about the fragility of humanity. I have to admit that at that time I was too young for a heavy theme like that. But when I began to visit them last month, I could still feel the same agitation I had felt twenty years ago, as if I were bumping into an old flame. So, I guess they are worth rewriting.

Q: Do you feel comfortable writing in English? Are there any challenges in terms of language?

A: I can't say that I'm more comfortable writing in English than writing in Chinese, but I'm never afraid of expressing myself in English. There are challenges, of course. The biggest challenge is how to choose the correct, yet stylish words. I find it an endless struggle, but that's the beauty of the art of language, isn't it? We would like to embrace this kind of challenge, right?

Q: Even if your mother tongue is Chinese, are there any times when you'd rather write in English than in Chinese? I ask, because I sometimes have the feeling that I'm stuck in between. I constantly find it difficult to write in English, but sometimes the problems just can't be resolved by turning back to Chinese. It's not like I could say it clearly in Chinese and then ask somebody to translate it into English. There are some things that I can't say in either language.

Q & A

A: I can't answer this question in general. All I can tell you is that when I want to write a funny story, I tend to write it in English. I guess it is because I listen to English every day. I have no idea how to write a funny dialogue in Chinese. But if I want to convey a sad mood, I can handle it better in Chinese. I published a novel, *Dreaming of a Return*, in 2013. It is a sad story about a female character's lost love during the journey of immigration. I wrote it in Chinese because my targeted readership is in China. I hope I can write more stories for English readers in the future.

Q: Please tell me who your favorite English writer(s) is(are).

A: It would be a long list. All the super names are on it. The two writers who actually influenced me the most are Joyce Carol Oates and Hemingway. Those are the two writers whose works I would read repeatedly.

Q: If you could choose freely, which country would you prefer to live in?

A: It would be a long list, too, running from France, Switzerland, England, Spain, to Israel, Iran, Vietnam, Thailand, and Mexico. I am currently living in America, where my career and family are based. I regularly visit China, where my father and my relatives live. But my heart has always been attracted by different cultures. I want to know people other than myself. I would regret leaving this world without fulfilling this dream.

FLOWERS BLOOM, FLOWERS FALL

by Ma Lan
Translated by Charles A. Laughlin

1

Women have been dying in our town, jumping off buildings, drowning, hanging, and poisoning themselves.

Four women have died, their ages between thirty-eight and twenty-three.

They died in place of me. The odor of death filled our Bent Neck town. Entertainment venues, like karaoke bars, quickly shut their doors. The streets were empty. Singing and dancing had long flourished in Bent Neck without being impacted by any deaths, even though people die all the time.

The people of our town had lived peaceful lives, waiting to live out our allotted years until the eternal sleep. The word "suicide" had been removed from *The People's Dictionary of Bent Neck*.

We had reason to believe that suicide was a thing of the past. The town's young and old, men and women, all stride forward, weathering all storms.

We had reason not to believe that death is right beside us, that death is inside the bodies of our loved ones, that death is a chronic disease just waiting for the time to be ripe, and that it can't be avoided. That no one can hold death back, or that it is like a broken sword thrust into our hearts, tearing us asunder.

I sat upright in my bed and turned my eyes outside the window. There were seven inches of snow. My mind was blurry white clumps as the snow was quavering on the tree branches. So much snow; this winter seemed to never end.

Every time you thought it was the last snowfall, it would again come falling from the sky.

In this snowy winter, as I recollected the dead women and sketched them out in my mind, I felt that they came into my body, gradually making me swell like a balloon getting bigger and bigger. Eventually, not being able to withstand the tension anymore, the balloon exploded with a pop in midair and its shreds scattered about. Some of the shreds fell into my computer. Chinese characters flashed across the screen like a group of dancing snowflakes; with no other place to go, they escaped into my fingertips.

I used both my hands to search for fire, wanting to melt the snow. Instead, I gradually became a flurry of snow with nowhere to run. I couldn't distinguish the dead women from me. Together, we formed gibberish symbols. I saw myself in a certain detail, and in the end I did not die, because they died.

One jumped from a building;

One swallowed sleeping pills;

One walked into a river;

One hanged herself.

The causes of death were various, but the common thing was that they all died.

Dead, yet they live today, and they don't think about the future. They are women I don't know, but they died. They were hurt by their feelings; in other words, they murdered themselves.

2

On the fifth of April, downy seeds fluttered and danced in the air. She didn't know what she was wearing when she jumped off the building. It was probably an ordinary floral print dress.

At the beginning of that day, she had no idea that she would end her life soon. Her husband told her to go buy some spicy boiled beef, thirteen yuan per serving. She had been to the neighborhood Sichuan restaurant ten times already this month.

Before they got married, she thought he wasn't particular about food, but that he just liked to drink. She didn't know how it started, but every few days he wanted some spicy boiled beef.

She suspected it was because of a woman, a lovely, little Sichuan girl. But she had no proof. Apart from his infatuation with spicy boiled beef, everything else was normal. His moves in bed were comfortable and orderly. His departure and return from work was like clockwork. He was a punctual man.

So what was it?

Her husband said, "It's just tasty, nothing more."

She didn't believe it could be so simple. Could life ever be that simple?

On the fifth of April, downy seeds danced in the air, making her heart flutter in a panic.

When she entered the restaurant, the owner came up to greet her and said, "We didn't buy any beef today. Would you like some spicy boiled pork?"

She was stunned. *There was no beef! How could there be no beef?*

The owner said she didn't know why; she went out early in the morning to shop, but Wang, the butcher at the wholesale market, said the beef was sold out, and he didn't know why everyone in town wanted beef either.

She was an easygoing woman, or you could say she didn't really care whether they had beef or pork.

She said, "Alright, pork then."

How could she have known her husband would be so sensitive about pork? He wasn't a Muslim, after all.

Her husband roared, "Why is this pork??"

She told him there was no beef, so they substituted pork, as if she was saying that there was no spring water, so they substituted distilled water.

But her husband exploded with rage, shouting, "This is an insane world, an insane restaurant, and insane spicy boiled pork! It doesn't make any sense!"

She said, "Why don't you eat something else?"

Her husband smiled coldly. "You're stupid; you used to be smart. If they don't have it, just don't buy anything! Why would you want a substitute? Substitutes are garbage! You can't have garbage in your life!"

She told him to keep it down—the neighbors would hear.

This made her husband shout even louder, "What are you afraid of? I just wanted to eat some spicy boiled beef and you came back with some spicy boiled pork. How do you expect me to deal with that kind of a shock?"

"What do you want, really?" She was at her wit's end.

Her husband said, "A divorce."

She said, "Okay."

Since her husband could bring up divorce on account of an order of spicy boiled beef, why couldn't she jump off a building on account of divorce?

She walked over to the restaurant building and jumped off.

Her body hit the ground. She was dead. The fluffy seeds were still swirling in the air. All the townspeople were under a shroud of fluffy seeds.

No one knew where her husband had gone.

3

Lili (assuming your name is Lili), you killed yourself by poisoning. Your lover broke off relations with you.

Relations? Once established, the possibilities of them breaking off ensues. The gates of hell are thrown open. The battle to the death begins, a battle with no smoking guns or outcry. If someone emerges from the battle alive, they live forever among the flames. After bandaging their wounds, they return to the battlefield, with lessons learned, maturing into invincible killers. Others become eternally seduced, and conquered.

For your part, you lay on the bed for an entire winter, designing your death, seeking a way out. Suicide would be the quickest method to save yourself. With a whoosh, as long as you have the technique down and the equipment ready, then you would never hurt again. What is the essential difference between living thirty years and living sixty years? There is none. There really isn't. All you do is to exhale more carbon dioxide and produce more waste.

You are unhappy. Happiness is a learned virtue, not something you can just catch onto without any guidance. You say that I am a responsible person; responsibility is like a warm hand in the winter. Some people say that taking a life is a sin. They say the ants you squash could be your ancestors. Therefore, if you kill yourself, you could very well be killing someone else. Everything is an illusion, a fabrication. You have nothing in your hands. Physical relations can only be resolved by physical means; when you destroy the body, the soul has no place to reside.

The heavy snow swirled. You are very hungry and made yourself some rice porridge. It was supposed to be the kind with chopped, preserved eggs in it. But you didn't find preserved eggs. They'd been eaten by the cat. You thought again of suicide. Only if you die, could you then be sure not to have to face him again. He couldn't possibly come looking for you. The word "impossible" represents a complete break, no hope.

How can a person go on living without hope? We all have that little bit of hope, or what strength would we have to rely on in order to cope with life?

He is still in your heart, like a dagger slicing your flesh. When you push the knife in hard, there is still no blood.

We can get into the details of your story. A year ago you were minding your own business on Wooden Nail Street in your hometown, like a pigeon or a chicken beside the road. You knew that spring in the south was moist and drizzly, and he appeared just at that moment, like a game piece falling into your palm, with a persistence that allowed no room for doubt. You couldn't call it fate because you had other options. You could have turned left and united happily with a guy who struck it rich. You could have turned right and stayed alone in an empty apartment, sprinkling perfume on a single bed. If you backed up a step, there were temples in which you could have left the mundane world and become a nun in a modern age. But instead,you went north with him. You were drunk with the excitement of taking a spontaneous journey with the brilliance of its immediacy. You needed that speed to illuminate your heart.

He said, "Let's get married next winter."

The promise was given.

The promise was a beautiful wreath placed around your neck.

Now he says that he wants a woman named Lili. Only Lili could give him love. You said, "My name is also Lili, from now on, I am Lili."

He said, "You're crazy. Women always go crazy." He went back to the south with Lili.

You knew that you were a narcissistic woman and he hated narcissistic women. He said narcissistic women all wanted to be raped by their fathers.

You strike a pose that you had never struck in your life. You put on a bridal gown. You paint your fingernails with nail polish so red that it is almost green. Your eyes seem to take flight. This is another side of you. When women use make-up they become a different woman, a woman whom they don't recognize. The woman in the mirror is another person, one who has never approached you. You look at her and know that extreme joy begets sorrow, that yin and yang interpenetrate.

You gaze at yourself in the mirror. You are transformed: colorful and radiant.

Go on living; all you have to do is to make one thing clear. Can't we just not make love with men? Isn't love just like a live fish? It certainly is not a dream. So let me have a dream for you, and your heart will be at peace If only there weren't those pesky men, we could go on living a happy life. Living is pretty simple after all. Living is instinctive to animals. Don't think that human beings are superior to animals.

No, father. Human beings are so superior that they can choose to kill themselves.

You move your hands, trying to prove that you still have the ability to caress. First you come close to his lips, but your hand loses its way in midair.

You understand, you're just not the type to be together with someone day and night. Once you start thinking about this, everything around you begins to change for a reason. Whatever you like just disappears, and even falls to the ground and shatters. For example, your jade bracelet. When you took a shower yesterday and were taking off your shirt, the shirt and the bracelet both dropped on the cement floor. The bracelet broke, and you watched it shatter into four pieces. Your gaze also shattered into four pieces. When the battle is lost it's like a mountain collapsing, legions of soldiers and horses piled in heaps. Dead bodies strewn over the fields. At this moment you are devastated; you can't protect the things you like, including the people you like.

I want to kill...myself.

You walk out the door and it is still snowing. You want to buy two bottles of Pepsi, so you walk to the 24-hour grocery store.

You see that crushed pigeon. Its grey belly is torn open with the insides coming out. Its head is lowered on one side. One car after another runs over the tiny body. The pigeon is innocent. All she did was walk on the motorway. She seems to be still alive; she is having some spasms. Another car is coming and you have no way to make it stop. People don't create a crime scene for a pigeon's death. What's the big deal? We're all going to die anyway.

Look for another man to sleep with and let him enter your body.

At 2:30am, you decide to make your move. He wants to leave you, so you can only poison yourself. It's just that simple, that blasé.

You leave a note for your landlord: *Don't be frightened. Inform my father that the bank account should go to him. This month's water and electricity payments are on the table.*

True, you have no compelling reason to die. Death does not

need a reason; looking for reasons is for logicians to do. You are not penniless, your CDs sell rather well. They say you're the singing star of the town, and the men are all secretly after you.

No one is openly after you, facing you with a big knife.

The tree behind your house split open yesterday.

A woman falls in love with a man. When the man has a change of heart and looks for someone new, he throws two women into a war. War kills people. Someone will die in this battlefield. The mission is accomplished only when blood is spilled. There is no other way out. No woman will break the siege intact.

The man had an affair. "Had an affair" is such an elegant phrase. It is charming and tender. The stench of blood will have to wait for time to stretch out its hands, and with a wave, it will come sooner or later.

4

No one knew why she was in the river.

For a middle-aged woman to be in the river, she had her reasons.

People said that she was unhappy because she lived alone. They said a woman was not complete without a man. A woman who had neither a man nor children was doomed.

She smiled calmly, knowing that these rumors were of no importance to her. The rumors didn't need to be challenged.

The moment she walked into the river, she didn't see the dead pigeon. Instead, she saw herself jumping off the third floor of a restaurant. She had some slices of meat in her hands and she was shrieking, "Why don't you have spicy boiled beef?"

What was the spicy boiled beef all about?

She noticed that the woman jumping off was naked. Her dress blew open in the air, fluttering to the ground like a flower wreath. The dress hit the ground the same time her body did. She must be in a vacuum, where everything falls at the same speed.

The woman who had jumped off the restaurant building was surrounded by a crowd. *When I die, I certainly don't want people crowding around me. I refuse any kind of relationship with an audience. People have no real relationships with each other anyway, even more so after death!*

Death is a kind of break-up with the world. You never speak to the world again.

She had had only one love affair. This man gave her the complete process of romance: longing, passion, jealousy, habit, disgust, and departure.

A man represented innumerable men. If you have seen a tree, you have seen the forest. You see water, it's an ocean; you hear the breeze, it is wind.

Life is between breaths, a slip of a boat passing through the fog.

Let us review the crime scene of several years ago. This scene is perhaps fabricated, just to make clear the male-centered society that she had experienced.

Consider the following case.

Sunday. They argued, about whether to go to his parents' house for Chinese New Year. His hollering made her dizzy. Her head was heavy and dizzy, like countless dancing maggots were in it.

He liked to eat steamed meat dumplings. She went to the nearby Shanghai restaurant and bought him dumplings with crab meat; she held the crab meat dumplings as if she were holding the hope for life.

These were shoddy dumplings. Small dumplings were supposed to be little balls with a point on the top, but these were flat, and when you bit into them your mouth was full of oily water. He blew up again.

"Why don't you just go home by yourself?"

"Threatening me?"

After the one and only break-up, she opened the drawer and discovered a love letter she had written to a female classmate when she was a teenager.

What else was there to say?

She changed the locks on the doors and put all of his things outside. Then she disinfected the whole apartment three times.

She requested time off from work and climbed over the mountains. The sky was blue and the sun was white.

She told the old priest that she wanted to become a nun, shave her head, and cultivate herself. She had had enough experience with carnal relations. Wealth and fame did not lure her anymore either, so all that was left was her religious faith. Her heart was still like a mirror and there was a look of kindness in her eyes. She would live a rustic, simple life.

She had become a vegetarian because without men she had lost her desire for flesh, but she wanted flowers in her room and she must be able to get online.

The old priest smiled and said, "You have not yet transcended the dusty, mundane world."

There is no dust in my eyes. They are brilliant as the morning sun.

The master, still smiling, said, "You, you take care of yourself."

She looked down at her own body. Her past desires had carried her into flight, making her unable to stop, bumping and bouncing different directions.

The master thought she was bowing to him so he folded his hands together and returned the bow, "If you feel anxious, you are welcome to return up the mountain."

She walked out the front door of the temple. The sky was empty. The landscape was like before, as it would be until it all fell apart.

Life could continue.

If she were thirty-eight, we could call her Lili. She worked as an assistant manager at a real estate company. Her monthly wage was 5,000 yuan. She filled her apartment with fresh flowers. Her little place was full of flower stands, alone and apart from the world. When she returned home, she would steep a pot of Biluochun tea and sink into a wooden chair. After a short rest, she put on a Bergman film. Life was nearly perfect.

It was Thanksgiving. Friends and family gathered over food and drink. The snow was so heavy, and the whiteness gave her a premonition of bad luck. She couldn't help it. She just had to leave.

She drove mindlessly to the lake, indifferent to everything. Her mother said she would move in with her in the summer. But did she need her mother? Her mother was so old that she barely recognized her. She missed the stewed red beans she ate on the mountain, and the green tea of the Tomb-sweeping festival.

She thought about taking a leave of absence from work and have a proper rest for a few years. She had enough money for her daily expenses. She didn't eat meat anymore and she didn't need to buy new clothes. Without living in a temple, she cultivated virtue alone in the city, rustic in the manner in which she ate and the way she dressed. Her physical desires receded and all men were like her brothers.

What did she need her mother for?

There was a swan on the lake. For a moment, she suspected that it looked more like a pigeon. *It could in fact have been the pigeon that was run over by me.*

FLOWERS BLOOM, FLOWERS FALL

That was an accident.

People found her car by the lake, and went on to find her body floating nearby in the lake. On the shore a few boats were pulled up. The weather was surely to blame, heavy snow covering the surface of the lake, as if there was solid ice underneath. She probably only wanted to get out of the car and enjoy the scenery.

They died. I lack the strength to go to heaven, not to speak of accurately chronicling them. How can you walk into the soul of one who has died? But I felt their pain, so real; I was in every scene, so real. I'm not sure if they are one person, or several people. Maybe they are me; actually, they are me.

A fish slipped and crawled up the bank. It peeled off its scales in front of everyone. She was certainly not taking it off for fame.

Who Is That? What Are They Doing?

One morning, I opened the door and found people and horses lined up for blocks, in groups of two.

We don't often see this in the town of Bent Neck. People used to gather on the street only for the purpose of gambling, but we banned gambling in Bent Neck fifty years ago, so big crowds disappeared altogether. Three's a crowd.

Over the past years, some gamblers couldn't take it, so they invented all sorts of novel ways to gamble. For example, you could bet on how many times you would blink in a minute, or whether the last digit on your car's license plate is odd or even.

I like a noisy crowd, just like the sunshine.

I forced myself into the crowd and asked, "What's going on?

Did they lift the ban on gambling?"

An old man said, "They're recruiting men for marriage! It's a cause for celebration!"

"Who's looking for a groom?"

"The village chief's daughter."

"Even the village chief's daughter puts out personal ads? She's only 28 years old!"

I circled round from the front to the back and discovered that there were both men and women, between the ages of 18 and 70, lining up. Our town may have banned gambling, but has started doing things like openly recruiting for spouses! But I still don't get it, what was the meaning of this? Clearly it was an omen of impending chaos.

"Are you going to buy meat or not? If not, what are you doing elbowing through here?"

"What? What do you mean buying meat?" I said.

"Are you kidding me or what? If you want to buy fresh meat you better get in line."

Apparently the old man was wrong about recruiting men for marriage; dream on!

I laughed and slowly made my way to the end of the queue, and whispered to the woman in front of me, "What meat can we buy here?"

"What are you talking about? I'm not buying meat! Stupid bitch!"

"Oh, well, then what is everyone lining up for? Don't be angry, I just don't know."

"My dad said the town was selling low-income housing, you line up here to get a house number. First come, first served."

"To get house numbers? That can't be right! My boss told me to come here to buy tickets for the football match against Straight

Neck Town."

"You really have a low IQ. This line is for getting your IQ score; the town has brought in the latest technology, which can determine your IQ with a blood test. People with an IQ lower than 80 will live on the west side. Those that score higher than 80 will live on the east side. If you have an IQ of 120 or over, you can live on the north side; it's really beautiful there."

"Humph! You think you know everything, don't you? Yes, we are lining up for a blood test, but it's to see whether you came in illegally or not. This technology can even indicate whether you intended to come in illegally or not. Because when you lie, your blood type changes."

It was all clear to me now; each person has his own soul.

Marriage licenses, meat, low income housing, tickets to football matches, blood test results...which one is the truth? Or is it nothing more than a magic act, or more likely a prank, so there is nothing going on at all, and these people in line are just passing along one falsehood after another?

I did not want to give up, though; I had to figure out what was happening in front of our house. I care about current affairs, just like I care about the weather!

I thought about those noble and respected people, those beautiful people, those people who shoulder the great burdens, those people at the front of the line, surely they would know the reason why this line exists?

Where did we come from?

"This is a secret, and you don't have the right to know," answered a man with three carrying poles on his left shoulder.

"Line up and you'll find out; young people are always trying to get something for nothing!" an older man kindly lectured me.

"I say we're getting fast tracked into the Party, do you believe it?" a fiery young guy answered.

By now I realized I could not get at the truth from other people's experiences, or know the origins of this event from the words of others. Each person has a secret.

I had to push my way up to the front and find out for myself. But the line seemed longer than ever, as if it had no end.

The main problem now was that a person suddenly appeared next to me, following me, talking to me....She looked exactly like me! Had I split into two?

Confused, I asked, who are you?

"I am Amy."

My name is Amy, too.

She said to me, "Your life is a total failure. Why don't you take a good look at yourself? You should change your lifestyle. You need a revolution, a revolution!"

"A revolution? Where would I start?"

"Start with yourself, put your fingers in the flame, and watch them burn."

I laughed, "You don't get it. I'm not going to burn my fingers. I'm trying to avoid pain. Can I burn down a building instead? I could reduce that tower in front of us to ashes."

"You don't have the courage; you won't even burn yourself."

"Amy, let's make a run for it!" I said. "We'll cross the river. Can you see? These are fallen leaves; these are flower blossoms. Autumn has come. This is our destiny!"

"Open your eyes and take a clear look, the people lining up have all disappeared. This is the falsity of life; how many illusions stand before our eyes?"

"They are there; don't you see the people?" I said, "It's only because in your heart you don't want to see them, so they don't exist."

"You have to understand fire; only when you understand fire, will you understand ashes."

"Amy, don't struggle with me. We have to love each other. I want to love someone so much....Could this be the unbearable weight of being they talk about?"

"I am yours. I am your other you. I am your heart." She said.

"Amy, let me caress you. Can I shoot you with a gun?"

"You can, but you will probably end up killing yourself; I'm afraid I'm bigger and stronger than you."

"Amy, tell me, why do they wait in line?"

"Think of it as a dream. All we face is each other, you and I, only you and I, and this building beneath us. We look down and see the bustling market square, and all the people almost like us. They experience the same pain we do, the same boredom. They are not any happier than we are, do you understand?"

"Amy, hold me tight, make me flat!"

Amy was gone. I found myself once again following an endless queue. I already lost my sense of direction, as if I kept going over the same spot, or going in circles.

I would never reach the truth; the truth was in the future.

But Amy, I need you, just like I need myself.

MA LAN was born in Meishan, Sichuan, China. Formerly an accountant at China Construction Bank, she immigrated to the U.S. in 1993. Since 1982, Ma Lan has published poetry, essays, and fiction in various Chinese literary journals. Her works have appeared in multiple annual anthologies. Her short story "Going Deaf" has been translated into German and Italian, and several of her poems in English appeared in *Poetry in Translation* (Summer 1996) and *Another Kind of Nation: An Anthology of Contemporary Chinese Poetry*, ed. Zhang Er and Chen Dongdong (New York: Talisman, 2008). Ma Lan has self-published a poetry collection *Zuozainali* (Where to Sit) and a short story collection *Hua Feihua* (Flowers Are Not Flowers). She has served for many years as an editor of *The Olive Tree* online literary magazine, the first online Chinese literary journal.

(From left to right) Charles Laughlin, Ma Lan, David Der-wei Wang, and Mingwei Song

CHARLES A. LAUGHLIN is the Ellen Bayard Weedon Chair Professor of Chinese Literature at the University of Virginia. Born in Minneapolis, he received his B.A. in Chinese Language and Literature from the University of Minnesota in 1988, and went on to complete a Ph.D. in Chinese Literature at Columbia University in 1996. He taught modern Chinese Literature at Yale University for ten years, and then served as Resident Director of the PKU-Yale Joint Undergraduate Program at Beijing University (2006-2007) and the Inter-University Program for Chinese Language Studies at Tsinghua University in Beijing (2007-2009). Laughlin's first book, *Chinese Reportage: The Aesthetics of Historical Experience*, was published by Duke University Press in 2002, with a Chinese translation forthcoming. He edited *Contested Modernities in Chinese Literature* (Palgrave Macmillan, 2005), and his latest book *The Literature of Leisure and Chinese Modernity* was published by University of Hawai'i Press in April 2008. Laughlin has translated Chinese stories, articles and poems for several collections, and his translations of Ma Lan's poetry have appeared in *Modern Poetry in Translation* and *Another Kind of Nation: An Anthology of Contemporary Chinese Poetry* (Ed. Zhang Er and Chen Dong. UK: Talisman House, Publishers, 2007).

Charles Laughlin with a visiting student from Tongji University

167

AN ONLINE CHAT
WITH MA LAN

Anna Wang Yuan discussed with Ma Lan about her story through WeChat, a popular social media platform in China. Below is the transcript from that discussion. It was translated into English by Anna Wang Yuan.

A: When editing your story, I found an interesting fact—you tend to juxtapose different times in the same story. For example, in "Who Is That? What Are They Doing?" you first described that "people and horses lined up," which gave me the impression that the story happened in a pre-automobile era. After that, you immediately mentioned that people like to bet on "whether the last digit on your car's license plate is odd or even." Why is that?

M: Wow, I've never thought about that.

A: I found it very interesting because it reminded me of my feelings when I immigrated from China to North America. At that moment, I felt that I had rushed forward twenty or even thirty years. Therefore, in my mind, time had been scrambled. I don't want to over interpret your work, but could you please tell me if you felt that way when you were writing your story?

M: You feel free to interpret it as you like. I don't mind. There are a thousand Hamlets in a thousand people's eyes.

A: Do you think that immigration has affected your writing?

M: I haven't really written about stories that happened in

168

America even though I have been living in the States for more than twenty years. Most of my stories are situated in China.

A: Most of your stories happen in a fictitious town called Bent Neck. At first, I thought this town was in America because the name, Bent Neck, gives me a strong feeling that it came straight out of a Western movie. Only after I'd finished reading the entire story did I realize that it was in China. Why did you choose the name, Bent Neck, for the town?

M: When I needed a town name, I instantly thought of the word "web". I translated "web" into Chinese by its pronunciation, "Wai Bo". Later, when Charles was translating my story into English, he translated "Wai Bo" into "Bent Neck" based on its meaning in Chinese.

A: What an interesting process! Let's talk about this town, Bent Neck. What is it like?

M: It's like a ghost town. Anything could happen in it. It is like the whole town is in an illusion.

A: I'd like to go back to the topic about how you scramble time in your stories. For example, there is an assistant manager working in a real estate company and a chief's daughter in one story. Do you think this kind of mix-matching has anything to do with your immigration experience?

M: I just invented a town. It is a virtual space. I allegorized my real experiences in life.

A: But I can't help but interpret it, or over interpret it. In China, I have friends who are about ten years younger than me. When we discussed Chinese movies, songs, or literature, I found that our age differences were a great factor in setting us apart. But when we talked about English movies, songs, or literature, I didn't feel that our age mattered that much. I think that's because in the 1980s, when China opened its door to Western literature and entertainment, all of us were on the same page, be it ten-years old or twenty-years old.

M: I see your point. In the 1980s, Chinese people were introduced to Western literature, films, and songs from different time periods all at once. Therefore, we weren't given enough time to soak them in, and associate them to our own experiences. We probably have the feeling of time being condensed and scrambled.

A: Does it affect the choice of time in your story? Like I said, when I immigrated from China to North America, I felt such a leap in time. It was like a great length of time was condensed into a blink. It was just like you met a village chief's daughter yesterday and see a real estate agent today, or you rode horses yesterday and drive a car today. Is that the way you thought of time when you wrote the stories?

M: It could be. If I were presented with many choices at the same time, I would have opted to ride a horse. Haha.

(Translated by Anna Wang Yuan)

A screenshot taken during Ma Lan's online chat with Anna Wang Yuan

RETURN TO GANDER

by Xiaowen Zeng

I saw the email from Gander, Newfoundland, Canada, by accident.

Since my son Nick started university in Michigan the previous year, the quietness of my home in the suburbs of Philadelphia had become almost unbearable. Driven by an urge for more video chatting time with him, I bought a Samsung phone that had a bigger screen than the Blackberry Torch I had been using. While setting it up at home, I was prompted to login to my Gmail account, which I hadn't used for a several years. I searched for the little black notebook where I had written down at least 30 passwords for various accounts. Like millions of others, I was living in a password jungle, worrying that one day I could lose access to everything in my life. Thank goodness I found the one for Gmail. The password was Beijing0903. Beijing was the city where I met Nick's father, Jing. September 3rd was Jing's birthday. I had loved him once. I knew that sooner or later a reminder would be thrown at me like a sharp flying knife in a Kung Fu movie and cut my heart wide open, but I never imagined that it could be an eleven-character password!

I logged in successfully. My Gmail account was full of spam like an abandoned garden hidden by weeds, but I spotted the email from a non-profit organization in Gander. In my mind, I saw a wild flower standing on a long beach and inhaled the refreshing breeze from the ocean. The email was an invitation to a memorial ceremony to commemorate the 10th Anniversary of the 9/11 terrorist attacks. Over 6,000 passengers on 39 planes were diverted to Gander in the wake of the 9/11 attacks and were sheltered by local residents. I was one of them. I spent four days in Gander, a small town with a population of about 10,000. I never knew this town existed before landing there. I had left my Gmail address with Aaron, a volunteer from a non-profit organization I met in Gander, so I was added to their mailing list. I learned from the emails that I received in the first couple of years that some passengers had returned to Gander. I may have promised Aaron that I would visit with my family, but I hadn't done so.

After 9/11, my employer let most foreign employees go, myself included. I couldn't find a job in the IT field. I started to work at a traditional Chinese medicine clinic during the day and bus tables in a restaurant at night to support Jing and Nick. Four years later, I had become a traditional Chinese medicine practitioner and acupuncturist. Jing finally got his Ph.D. and was offered a job in China. Nick was twelve that year. As an ABC (American Born Chinese), his system had rejected the Chinese language as well as dumplings. I had tried very hard to tutor him in Chinese, but he could hardly make a meaningful sentence. Jing and I decided that I'd better stay in the U.S. so Nick could continue going to school. We promised ourselves that once Nick started university, we wouldn't suffer the separation one more day and would live together in China forever. Jing ended up being one of the most accomplished astronomers in China. He was overwhelmed by the media's attention and acted like a star. Two months before Nick headed off to university, a rumor started to spread that my husband was having an affair.

I had moved more than fifteen times in a decade, for better or worse, due to all the changes in my life, so it seemed normal that my departure led to a permanent farewell to Newfoundland. I'd had enough battles to fight. I was too tired to manage even two personal email accounts. I had lost my connection with Gander.

Staring at the new phone for quite a while, my room was already wrapped in huge and heavy shadows. I felt as if I were sitting in a collapsed and dark mine, dying for blue sky and fresh air. As I recalled, there was no shortage of blue sky and fresh air in Gander. It struck me that the four days I had spent there was a turning point for me. What got diverted was not only my trip, but also my life. It was only one week away from September 11th. I'd never planned a trip in such a short amount of time—I normally had to plan to be spontaneous! I surprised myself by accepting the invitation.

The flight felt shorter than I had expected. I arrived at the Gander airport terminal, the same place I was ten years ago. In late August 2001, I was sent by my employer, a high tech company in Dallas, to Paris on a business trip. On September 11th, I boarded the return flight and couldn't wait to get home. Nick had been suffering from the stomach flu. Jing got high grades as a Ph.D. student, but he was not a qualified caregiver. Friends joked that he couldn't even boil water. It seemed to me that science was, and would always be, his first love. Care of the household and the upbringing of Nick fell to me even when I was busy with work. The flight was in the air, over the Atlantic Ocean, when the U.S. airspace was hurriedly shut down. After sitting in the plane for over twenty hours, including over fourteen hours on the tarmac in Gander, while being cut off from the outside world, I teetered on the edge of a mental breakdown. I was scheduled to attend a security system steering committee meeting on September 12th. It was my first chance to be appointed as a project manager, but I missed it completely. The flight captain finally told everyone what had happened that morning. Some passengers cried since they knew people who worked in the World Trade Center. The woman next to me worried about who would look after her children if she didn't get home on schedule. I was shocked and fell into a deep pond of sadness because of the loss of human lives. We finally disembarked. I only had what I carried, and I had little sense of where I was, or where I was going. My mind was so occupied that I didn't pay attention to my surroundings. I tripped over the foot of a steel chair in the terminal and yelled out in pain. I drew a lot of attention. A white guy in a cotton short-sleeved shirt and a pair of shorts came over. He introduced himself as Aaron. He told me that he was a volunteer helping the stranded passengers. He offered to take me to a clinic. I noticed that his hair was the color of chocolate and his eyes were like jade. He extended his strong arm to me and almost carried me to his blue Ford SUV.

Now, ten years later, here was Aaron again. He was greeting a couple of passengers. I still recognized his straight back from a distance. He was again in a short-sleeved shirt and a pair of shorts. Meanwhile, I had wrapped myself in a long sweater. I felt self-conscious about my appearance. Over the past couple of years, I had lost weight and my once clear, bright eyes were cloudy with wrinkles starting to creep in. I had also cut my long, thick hair short. He turned around and his eyes met mine. I was pleased that he still recognized me. He came over with a smile. The air was frozen for a few seconds, waiting for ten years of vicissitudes to pass. He had obviously put on a few pounds and his hair was now like salt and pepper. While time had left its trace on his appearance, it had also brought an intriguing maturity. I swore I saw some sadness in his eyes. I became curious about what had happened to him in this small, quiet community.

He finally said "give me a hug" and touched my back with his warm "bear hands". Comforted by their warmth, I wished his hands could stay for a little bit longer. He commented that I looked the same as I did ten years ago. That was a sweet lie. He offered to drop me off at the motel his family once owned. I followed him to a used pickup truck. I asked him where his blue SUV was.

"Oh, right, you once cried in that blue SUV," he teased.

His ex-wife had taken the blue SUV, along with their daughter, to Toronto a few years ago. She wanted a different life. But for him, leaving the home where his family had lived for generations would have been as painful as digging out a huge tree root by hand. He said it in a calm voice as if telling someone else's story. In his truck, he took a photo out of his wallet and showed it to me. It was his daughter. She was a cute seven-year-old girl. As he was inserting the photo back inside his wallet, I noticed that his fingers trembled a bit. I immediately recognized a sign of ongoing pain resulting from a shattered family.

I had cried in his blue SUV ten years ago. He had taken me to the local clinic to see Dr. Morris after I twisted my left ankle. Dr. Morris, a fine older woman with white hair, kept calling me "poor sweetie". She wrapped an elastic bandage from my toes to my mid-calf to prevent swelling. She also prescribed some painkillers. In the end, she didn't charge me anything since I was a stranded passenger. Once Aaron helped me back to his SUV, I collapsed and let my tears run all over my face. I was in pain. I was away from home, and I was fearful of an uncertain future. When would I return home, and what would happen to my career as a result of my missed meeting? He told me to take a deep breath and then count

175

from one to ten. I did; I counted to one-hundred. Then he took me to where twelve other passengers from all over the world were already settling in.

Now, sitting in Aaron's truck, I looked out the window and saw many bright houses glimmering in the sunlight. Their colors were the same as the wild flowers in Newfoundland—green, red, yellow, and purple.

"The colors of those houses are beautiful!" I said.

"I painted them."

"Really?" I replied. "I thought you were running a motel."

"When my ex-wife and I separated, I couldn't afford to buy her out, so I took a job as a handyman." There was more pride than sorrow in his tone.

"And what about you, what have you been up to?" Aaron asked.

I told him about my job, but I left out any details about what had happened to me personally.

After I checked in at the motel, Aaron and I sat across a picnic table and had a glass of lemonade. The fresh air blew on my face and reminded me of baby Nick's kiss. I wondered if it was the sky making the sun brighter or if it was the sun making the sky bluer. It was a moment of perfection. I told Aaron that I moved from Dallas to Philadelphia a few years ago and there were some unexpected changes in my life. Too soon, Aaron had to go back to the airport to pick up more passengers, but he said that he would like to catch up later. He invited me to his house for a kitchen party the next day.

The next day, I attended the 9/11 memorial ceremony at the town square. People from all over the world attended. I was pleased that I was able to witness the kindness and humanity of Gander residents, which lighted the cold and dark night along with them.

RETURN TO GANDER

A piece of steel from the World Trade Center was presented to the town. The U.S. Ambassador to Canada spoke of the tireless efforts of the community. He said the motto of Gander could be "Without Waiting to be Asked". I realized that I had been expected to be many people's rock. Even before my husband and son, there were my siblings. My mother died when I was twelve and being the oldest, I had helped raise my brother and sister. I had lived up to everyone's great expectations. Then, purely arranged by fate, I actually exposed my vulnerability and was taken care of while I was in Gander. To me, this was almost revolutionary. Aaron had been busy the whole time, so I only got a chance to say "hi". For some reason, standing in the crowd with thousands of people, but knowing he was around, was comforting.

Aaron's house seemed smaller and older compared to the one in my memory, but it was still cozy. A new piece of art on the wall, one that wasn't there ten years ago, caught my eye. It was a mosaic comprised of small pieces of china, in a wooden frame. Aaron told me that his ex-wife had broken an antique Dutch vase while arguing with him. He glued the pieces into the shape of a blue flag iris.

"Sometimes we have to learn to turn a shattered dream into a piece of art," he said. The kitchen was packed with over thirty people. Half were locals, the other half were visitors. Aaron teamed up with three guys and sang a few Newfoundland folk songs, *We'll Rant and We'll Roar, The Star of Logy Bay,* and *Tribute to Newfoundland*, while playing guitar and mandolin. After the performance, Aaron was offered a glass of screech by a curly haired guy, but turned it down since he had been sober for a couple of years. The curly haired guy insisted and made fun of him. I grabbed the glass and drank it although I was never a drinker. After a few glasses of screech, along with kissing a codfish on the mouth, all the locals in the kitchen accepted me as an "Honorary Newfie" and invited me to join the boat tour Aaron organized for the morning. They planned to depart from Little Harbour on Gander Lake. I told them that I already booked a flight to Philadelphia. Everyone sighed with disappointment. Aaron looked unhappy, but not surprised.

My head started to spin. I needed air. I left the kitchen and walked to the porch. I took a seat on a wooden bench. Aaron brought a cup of tea and sat next to me. I began to talk. I talked as if I had been locked up in solitary confinement for years and was finally free.

After I learned of Jing's affair, I had rushed back to China to rescue my marriage. I hardly recognized Jing in his Hugo Boss suit and with his hair dyed black. Jing's young lover hit the roof after finding out that he lied about his marital status. She posted a long article on her blog revealing some juicy details about their affair, details like those usually found in erotic novels. She also admitted that she had accepted Jing's gift of an expensive condo, where she had given birth to Jing's daughter! Her blog got a million hits overnight and thousands of comments. Scandal on the Internet had become a new drug in Chinese society. I was stunned by the news of Jing's illegitimate daughter and his unexplained income. It was as if Jing had drunk a magic potion and turned into a different creature, one I didn't know. I felt that I was exposed and naked in public every single second, but that was only the beginning of the nightmare. Jing was reported to have plagiarized another scientist's research paper, which crushed any remaining trust I had in him. It seemed millions of people supported my idea of divorce. Success was a still a public affair, but failure was no longer a private funeral. It took a record two short weeks to get a divorce. The local court opened especially for me on a Sunday!

RETURN TO GANDER

I was amazed that I told Aaron my whole story in under an hour. He touched my hair gently and looked at me with understanding in his eyes. Yes, understanding, not cheap sympathy, something new to me. In that moment, it seemed all of the struggles, anger and tears became as light as puffin feathers.

In the morning, I decided to delay my flight home and go to Little Harbour. I heard my heart beating and I felt like a school girl escaping from long and boring classes. I could really use another diversion in my life. Aaron was already on the boat along with the others. They were getting ready to sail. He smiled at me with a pleasant look of surprise and extended his hand.

He said, "Hop on!"

XIAOWEN ZENG was born and raised in Jiamusi, China. She received a M.A. in Literature from Nankai University, China, and a M.S. in IT from Syracuse University, U.S.. She currently works as an IT director in Toronto, Canada. As a prolific Chinese writer, she has published three novels, a collection of short stories and novellas, and a collection of essays. She also has more than three hundred pieces of short stories, essays, and poems published. She is a produced screenwriter too. She won a Central Daily News Literature Award in 1996, a United Daily Literature Award in 2004, a Chinese Writers Erduosi Literature Award, and a Zhongshan Cup Overseas Chinese Literature Award in 2011. In 2014, she was awarded the top prize at The First Global Chinese Prose Competition. Her works have been included in multiple literature collections. Her short story "The Kilt and Clover" was ranked in the Top 10 by the China Fiction Association in 2009. She served as the Vice Chair and Chair of the Chinese Pen Society of Canada from 2004-2012.

Xiaowen Zeng signing books at China's 22nd Book Expo

Q & A
WITH XIAOWEN ZENG

Anna Wang Yuan asked Xiaowen Zeng seven questions after reading her story, "Return to Gander".

Q: Would you tell me briefly about your education background and immigration story?

A: I received a M.A. in Literature from Nankai University, China in 1991. I moved to the U.S. in late 1994 and earned a M.S. in Information Technology from Syracuse University in 1998. In 2003, I moved to Toronto, Canada, and became a Canadian citizen in 2007.

Q: You have a full-time job as an IT director, and you write during your spare time. How do you balance your job and passion?

A: I have to admit that it has been challenging to hold a stressful job and find time to write. I have been trying to write whenever I have a little spare time. I have written in all kinds of places—on a train, in an airplane, on a beach while vacationing, or while at a clinic waiting to see a doctor. In a way, the logic and coolness of an IT director and the dreaminess and the emotion of a writer makes my life unique.

Q: You are a prolific writer. Would you tell me more details about your literary works?

A: My first piece of writing got published in 1991. Since then, I have published three novels: *The Daytime Floating Journey*, *The Night Is Still Young*, and *The Immigrant Years;* a collection of short stories and novellas called *The Kilt and Clover*; a collection of essays called *Turn Your Back to the Moon*; and more than three hundred other short stories, essays and poems. My literary works have been included in a number of literature collections.

My short story, *"The Kilt and Clover"*, was on the China Fiction Association's Top 10 List for 2009. I co-wrote with Sun Bo a twenty-episode TV drama titled *Invented in China*, which won a Chinese Writers Erduosi Literature Award and a Zhongshan Cup Overseas Chinese Literature Award in 2011. It has recently been made into a thirty-three-episode TV series retitled *Let Go of Your Hand*.

I received the top prize in the First International Chinese Prose Competition awarded in China in November, 2014. The competition featured several hundred entries from around the globe. Other awards I won include a Central Daily News Literature Award in 1996 and a United Daily Literature Award in 2004.

Q: What response did you receive from Chinese readers?

A: I attended two book launches in China. The first one was in Beijing, China, for my novel, *The Daytime Floating Journey*. The second one was in Ha'erbin, China, for my novel, *The Night Is Still Young*. I received warm response from readers on both occasions. My novel, *The Immigrant Years*, was selected by China's 22nd Book Expo in Sanya, Hainan Province as the feature release/book signing on the opening day. Right after winning the prose competition in 2014, Chinese national television network, China Central Television, produced a short documentary about me, which was screened in China and Toronto, Canada. Also, there have been a number of literature research papers and reviews about my works.

Q: I've read that your novel, *The Immigrant Years*, had been selected as required reading by the University of Toronto. Would you tell me more details?

A: It was selected by the English/Chinese Translation (ECT) Program at the Centre for French and Linguistics at University of Toronto at both the Mississauga and Scarborough campuses as required reading for 2015 and 2016. In 2015, I was invited to make a presentation and share the creation process with the students.

I have also given readings at York University and Western University in Canada, and at Jinan University and other schools in China.

Q: As far as I know, "Return to Gander" is the first short story you wrote in English. What made you decide to start creative writing in English?

A: I would love to introduce my writing to the English world. I tell stories about immigrants who left China in the late 1980s and planted their roots in North America. Their love, marriages, and friendships are filled with joy and tears. They share common accomplishments and struggles, but each of the stories is unique in its own way. I believe my works would contribute to the grand narratives of human migration.

Q: You are a pretty versatile writer. You have published fiction and non-fiction, prose and poems, and you also have movie/TV scripts that have been produced. How do you decide what format to use before you start?

A: In most cases, a lead character shocks or moves me and follows me for days and nights until I start writing about him/her. Once I sit down in front of my computer, I listen to my instinct. If I hope to focus on the character's psychological landscape, I would write a fiction piece. If the dramatic scenes happening between the characters attract me, I would choose to tell the story visually and write a movie/TV script. I am a writer without any restrictions.

Xiaowen Zeng at the book launch of her novels, *The Daytime Floating Journey* and *The Night Is Still Young* in China in 2009

ABOUT THE EDITOR

Anna Wang Yuan is a Chinese Canadian novelist and translator. She was born and raised in Beijing, China, and immigrated to Canada in 2006. She is the author of four novels and one short story collection in Chinese. She is also the Chinese translator of Alice Munro's *The View from Castle Rock*. Her latest publication is *Beijing Women: Stories* (translated into English by Colin S. Hawes and Shuyu Kong. Portland: Merwin Asia, 2014). She is currently living in Irvine, California.

Also by Anna Wang Yuan
Beijing Women: Stories
(translated by Colin S. Hawes and Shuyu Kong.
Portalnd: Merwin Asia, 2014)

Printed in Great Britain
by Amazon